To A Very Esteemed Professional that I enjoy working with; Angela Holmes. Thanks! for all of the laughs that keeps my mue flowing! and most importantly thanks for marriage advice. Most importantly thanks for supporting my writing Career :)

God Bless,

P. D. Carter
1/8/08

REAL WOMEN DON'T WEAR PINK

by
P. D. Carter

1663 Liberty Drive, Suite 200
Bloomington, Indiana 47403
(800) 839-8640
www.AuthorHouse.com

© 2005 P. D. Carter. All Rights Reserved.

No part of this book may be reproduced, stored in a retrieval system, or transmitted by any means without the written permission of the author.

First published by AuthorHouse 12/22/05

ISBN: 1-4259-0483-1 (sc)

Library of Congress Control Number: 2005910876

Printed in the United States of America
Bloomington, Indiana

This book is printed on acid-free paper.

"Think of life as a tunnel; you're only going through."

*This book is dedicated to my beloved grandmother, Pearline M. Carter.
May she rest in peace.
And to my loving daughter, Jayla Renee. Dream big and maximize your
success. Momma won't always be around to pick you up by your bootstraps.*

ACKNOWLEDGEMENTS

First and foremost, I would like to thank God for everything that He's done and everything He has in store for me. This may be a short book, but it has a message. It's the first, but not the last. Trust me, there's more to come. I would like to thank my readers for supporting me. And for those of you who are just as excited about the book as I am: here it is. I would like to thank the Author House staff for such an exciting publishing experience. God said it, I claimed it, and it is so!

1
BUSINESS MEETS PLEASURE

Oh, my God. I can't feel my legs. Where am I? Am I dead? Okay, okay calm down Rita. What's the last thing that you can remember? Think girl, think. I came home from shopping and Jeff started an argument. Then he pushed me on the ground. After that… umm… Damn. Oh yeah! That son-of-a-bitch hit me on my head with a lamp. So what in the hell happened after that? Did he kill me?

"Rita, baby, it's momma. Can you hear me baby?"

That's my momma. I can hear her but why can't I open my eyes? I can't see her. I can't say anything to her.

"Rita, baby, please wake up. I need you. Sarah needs you. Please. Wake up."

I could hear my mother weeping nearby. I can even feel her tears trickling down my hand. It feels different, though. Not like teardrops or even water. More like a cool touch or breeze brushing my hand. So why is that? Why does everything feel and sound so distant? I guess I'm not dead because I'm neither in heaven or hell right now. Am I in a coma? That's got to be it. I'm in a coma.

"Hey mommy. Hey mommy. I miss you. I miss you."

My baby girl. Oh how could I have left her all alone? I've never heard her sound so sad before. She will never understand what her daddy did to me. How could he? My own husband. I should have seen it coming. All of the fighting and bickering. It was bound to happen one day. I wish that I had never met him. Unfortunately he was so damn charming. I'll never forget the day we met....

"Can I get you anything else, Ms. Wilkins?" said the slightly slim waitress with the platinum blonde highlights.

"No. That will be all, thank you. You may bring the bill."

After a few minutes I noticed that the young waitress was taking her time returning with the bill. I was in a bit of a hurry and I didn't feel like waiting. I grabbed my purse and headed towards the hostess.

"Excuse me. I sent my waitress for the bill and she never returned. I'm in a bit of a hurry and I'd really like to just pay my bill and go." I was a bit disturbed and irate at this moment.

"I don't know what could be taking her so long. I'll check in the back. Excuse me for a moment."

Shortly after, a tall, medium build, gentleman with short hair returned with the hostess.

"I do apologize for your wait Mrs.?"

"Wilkins. Rita Wilkins," I said with a flirting smile. "And you are?"

"Jeff Bridges. I'm the manager of this fine establishment. Did you enjoy your meal?" His deep tones made my soul shake.

"Delightful. But I'm in kind of a hurry and I just want to pay my bill and go."

"Well your meal's on the house, Mrs.?"

"Ms. Wilkins. The only Mrs. Wilkins that I know is my mother."

"Well Ms. Wilkins, like I was saying. The meal's on the house if you promise to return here for dinner tomorrow night."

I couldn't resist his offer, considering he was so damn fine. Although he had on a blazer you could still see his muscles bulging out. I wanted to do him on the spot, but unfortunately I had to play hard to get. I mean, come on. What kind of girl do you think I am?

"Maybe. I'll have to check my schedule. If I'm available, you'll see me. But if not, it's been a pleasure Mr. Bridges."

"Pleasure's all mine Ms. Wilkins." He opened the glass door for me and watched closely as I exited on the patio.

The day was warm and sunny. I had worn the perfect lavender dress that cut right above the knee. Sexy, but not too flashy. Perfect for my two o'clock conference. The white straw hat with the lavender band

and bow complemented my dress well. I must say that with the pearls, purse and shoes accentuating the ensemble; I was a well-put together sister. Truth be told, I was merely a rookie in the corporate world. A child dressed in grown folks clothes. I was fresh out of college and doing pretty well for myself. I decided to put off grad school for a while due to the fact that I landed a hot little position as marketing manager for Candy Records.

Sad to say, but I truly believe that I was hired for my cute face and shapely figure. The CEO of the company complimented me more on my hair and nails than he did on my scholastic achievements. Hey, it's a dog-eat-dog world out there and I had bills. So what's a girl to do? That's right; I hemmed all my skirts up two inches and marched my cute ass into my new office the next day. Oh, like you wouldn't do it! Needless to say, it did the trick and here I am on an all expense paid trip to New Orleans. Twenty- three years old, no kids and doing it! Did I mention that my condo was company owned? The rent I paid was like being on Section 8 with luxury amenities. And the company car, uh! Back in Chicago, the cops pull me over daily because something's got to be fishy about a 23 year-old driving a brand new Mercedes with plates that read "Candy 4 U".

After running the plates and checking my company I.D. it all made sense. Let's face it; it all does seem a little surreal. To this day, it still seems a little hard to believe. This wasn't my first business trip. I had traveled twice prior to this and my boss felt that I represented the company well. Who knew? My parents were very proud and supportive. They were even more glad that they didn't have to help me pay back all of those student loans. So I guess it worked out for everyone.

So here I am presenting in front of thirteen potential investors. None of which have chocolate faces, mind you. Sometimes the best part of your job can be the worst part as well. I popped my collar to the fact that I was the youngest woman at the record label. But when I solely had to market the label, miles and miles away, to old, white faces; suddenly it was not so appealing. Overall, I toughed it out and thought about all the money I was making. Sure, a sixty-five thousand dollar salary may not be a lot for you, but for a twenty-three year old college grad, huh. Need I say more?

"So in closing Candy Records will undeniably be a great asset and I assure that you won't be disenchanted. Any questions?" I sweated my way through yet another great presentation and once again convinced the investors to advance their money into Candy Records. So that's what I did. I lived well, ate well, rode in luxury and traveled: all for one or two presentations a month. Of course I went into the office daily, but only to check my messages, sit at a desk and drink coffee. It was more like a social than work. Although I initially applied for a position in the finance department, this turned out to be more fun.

So my workday was over and I still had five days left in New Orleans. I always try to land the deal in a day or two so that I can vacation the other days. The only disadvantage to traveling was that I always traveled alone. My friends and family were back in Chicago and I had no one to keep me company. I was starting to get accustom to being alone. This allowed me to open up and meet more people. So I vowed to make a new friend every time I traveled. Maybe this time my new friend will be Mr. Bridges.

I was eager to see him again but I didn't want to seem desperate. Besides, if he was on the day shift this morning; he probably wouldn't be there this evening. So I decided to go shopping. Malls had become my companion while on the road. I had a lot of free money considering the company paid the majority of my bills. I had my own style and was sort of sophisticated with my apparel. As a result of this, I shopped at a lot of boutiques. One of the greatest advantages to traveling was that no one in Chicago had on the same thing. Besides, everyone my age was wearing jeans, tees and athletic wear. I've never been a gym shoe creeper myself.

Because of my profession, and maturity level, I wore a lot of dresses and suits. Even my casual wear was a bit classy. People often mistook my age for early to mid-thirties. I wonder how old Mr. Bridges thought I was. I wonder how old he is. Normally I would only date guys older than me. Late twenties, early thirties. Twenty-three year old boys in Chicago just don't have it together. I'm sure there's a handful like myself but the others just can't keep up. They're either standing on the corners pushing dope or still living with their mommas. Or both! Besides, this is a very critical point in my life considering most men would try to use me for what I have anyway.

After a full day of shopping, I finally retired to my room. Traveling with all of those new clothes was out of the question. So what I do is pack them up and mail them to my mom back in Chicago. This allowed me to build my wardrobe and be creative in my style. I had chosen the perfect outfit to wear to dinner the next night. I was prepared to knock Jeff's socks off.

I retired for the evening in hopes to wake up vibrant and refreshed. The next morning was a little cool. I had coffee on the balcony and watched the clouds roll in. It felt so good to just relax and enjoy life. The summer days were long and lazy. I sometimes find myself jaded and bored. This was certainly a lazy day. The air was crisp and you could smell the rain approaching. Days like this were ideal for spending time alone. After getting dressed, I decided to go downstairs to the gym for a morning workout. The gym was full of bodybuilders and show-offs. I'm not the athletic type but I work out here and there to maintain my figure. I was all breasts and butt, no belly. My legs and thighs were meaty but not fat. No flab or cellulite on me, baby.

"Hey little lady. How ya' doing today?" A short, over-muscular man asked from behind. He hadn't even seen my face yet so I assumed he was talking to my ass and not me.

"I'm fine and you?" I always responded with my serious, professional voice when I didn't want to be bothered.

"I didn't ask you how you looked; I asked you how you were doing."

Oh please. As if that line ever worked on anyone. It amazes me how guys can see that you're way out of their league but try to holler anyway. I give him a big NO for effort. Come on. He was like twice my age and I could have sworn that he was missing a tooth in the front of his mouth. Now don't get me wrong, I'm not arrogant by a long shot. But when you know you're a hot commodity, you have to be careful with who you engage.

I've come across some real monkeys so far and I just want to be careful with whom I mingle. For all I know, this could be my future baby-daddy. I'm young, but I do have my priorities in order. And sleeping with a snag-a-tooth, church deacon, who thinks he's sexy, is not my style. So when it's all said and done, Rita thinks with her mind and not her booty. But, the booty does get lonely sometimes. What?

I'm twenty-three. I'm young and impressionable baby. Single and loving it. You know!

After an hour's workout, I was pretty hungry. I showered and headed down to the corner café. Afraid that it might rain, I dressed in khaki slacks and an orange sweater. My short cut had sweated out from the workout so I flopped a khaki, fitted baseball cap on my head.

"Welcome to Sergio's. My name is Jeff and I'll be your server this morning. Are you ready to order Ms. Wilkins?"

What are the odds? Here I am looking like *who did it*, and Jeff Bridges is my server. Of all mornings, why this one?

"So are you stalking me or is this like a part-time job for you?"

"I'm stalking you." He smiled and his mouth full of pearly whites enticed me.

"No, I'm just kidding," he continued. "I run this restaurant too. I saw you walk in and told your server that I would take this one. So, we meet again Ms. Wilkins."

"Rita. Please."

"Well Ms. Rita. May I join you for breakfast?"

"No. You may take my order, server. I'll have the Italian omelet and regular coffee. And oh yeah, I like my coffee black and strong. Like the cowboys make it."

He smiled and proceeded to submit my order. The order returned with orange juice instead of coffee. I stopped him dead in his tracks.

"Excuse me, waiter." I could tell that he didn't appreciate my disdain.

"I asked for coffee, not orange juice."

"I thought that orange juice would be a little more age appropriate. I need to see some I.D. for coffee: especially cowboy coffee. How old are we again?"

Oh, we have a comedian on our hands. A real *ha-ha* man, huh?

"How old did you assume I was?"

"Oh about, nineteen or twenty."

"Well I guess that would make you a real pervert, huh, Mr. Bridges? You did, in fact, ask me out for dinner tonight. Didn't you?"

"Oh you were obviously mistaken Rita."

"Oh, I'm Rita now?"

"I merely asked you to dine at my restaurant again. I ask all of my customers to dine with us again."

I was affronted and appalled that he would respond in such a tone. How dare he? Sadly, his rudeness made him even more appealing to me. I was still determined to show up at the restaurant that evening.

"You obviously don't know who you're messing with, Mr. Bridges. So I'm going to overlook your insolence and act as if none of this ever occurred. Now, if you will, bring me my coffee and let me enjoy my breakfast or I'm going to have to put in a complaint to the owner."

"As you wish Ms. Wilkins." He smiled flirtingly and returned shortly after with the coffee that I initially ordered. Jeff smiled and lightly brushed my hand as he pulled away from the coffee mug.

"Enjoy your meal Ms. Wilkins." Why is this man so damn fine? All I want to do is work and travel, but oh no, there just had to be that one thing to intervene. As much as I wanted to avoid this man, I couldn't resist. There was something about him: other than being fine!

Later that evening I prepared for dinner in hopes that Jeff would be there. I dressed in my little, red dress that accentuated my breast and hips. Earlier I stopped by the salon to touch up my haircut. I'm not the one for make-up but I felt a need to go all out tonight. Nineteen or twenty? Huh. Just wait. He'll be kissing my pumps by the end of the night.

After glossing my lips and misting on some perfume, I was ready. My red stilettos that laced up my legs really set the outfit off. I walked into the restaurant confident that I would knock him dead. Hell I was looking good, smelling good and probably tasting good if he wanted to find out. I had been alone for three months and out of town for a week. Hell, I was hornier than a paraplegic who could get it up for the first time in nine years.

I was surprised when another young man took my order. He was young, around my age. Cute, but he was no Jeff Bridges.

"Dining alone today?" the young waiter asked.

"No, I'm waiting for someone." Did I sound desperate or what? There was no guarantee that this man was going to show up. Two hours later his absence proved this to be true.

"Shall I bring your bill or are you still waiting for the other party to join you?"

"You may bring the bill." I was so embarrassed. How could I be such a fool? Here I am, all dolled up, and for what? Nothing. After dinner I decided to walk to the hotel instead of taking a cab. The rain had died town and the streets weren't that slick. When I got to the hotel, I sat on the stoop for a while. Gazing up at the moon, I realized that my lavish lifestyle was not a happy one. Sure I made good money and had a lot of freedom on the job, but money can't buy everything. It sure couldn't buy me love. It wasn't so much that I missed my family back home. It was just that I was ready for a family of my own. Dating and living the single life wasn't my thing. I wanted to be settled.

As I opened the door to my room, I gasped in amazement. There were rose petals and candles all over. The tub was filled with hot bubble bath and a bottle of champagne chilled nearby. There was a small gift box on the bed with a red ribbon and bow. Attached was a note that read, "Sorry I missed you Ms. Rita. Please accept this peace offering and join me for breakfast in the morning. See you at eight. You know the place." I opened the box and there was a white gold watch, with diamond accents; and yes, it was real! Underneath the watch was another note that read, "Don't be late."

Was this man for real? I hope he didn't steal it because I was definitely wearing that bad boy the next day. But how did he know where I was staying? I called down to the concierge to see if he had any information. He informed me that a gentleman had everything ordered to the room. He also threw in that Jeff was a good tipper.

Needless to say, Jeff definitely wanted some booty and was willing to pull all the tricks to get it. I like it in him. Okay, so of course I had to go through the whole routine the next morning. Unfortunately, an after five dress was inappropriate for the occasion, so I had to dig deep into my wardrobe for this one.

The next morning I was up bright and early. I got a workout in to get my adrenaline flowing. It was an extremely hot day so I dressed in a long white sundress that was split to the thigh on each sides of the dress. It was a halter dress that cut down to the small of my back, so of course I wasn't wearing a bra. Didn't need one. I have no children so my breasts were still high and perky. The halter draped low in the front, so I had the puppies out for the day. It was all about sex appeal baby. Jeff wasn't the only one with a few tricks up his sleeve. Only difference is; I didn't have to pay for mine.

As I exited the lobby I realized that I didn't know which restaurant to meet him at. I took my chances and waited at the café on the corner.

"May I take your order Ms. Rita?" Oooh wee. No this man did not have his chest out. Hurt me, hurt me. At that moment I felt like the goofy dog with bulging eyes in the cartoons. You know, the one sitting at the dinner table whistling and raving over the sexy song stress. Is you is, or is you ain't my baby? He wore a pair of nice, black, linen slacks with a black linen shirt to match. But best of all, the shirt was unbuttoned and he had on a white tank underneath.

"You may not." I responded. "But you may join me for breakfast."

As he pulled the seat from under the table, I noticed that he was wearing black sandals. What? No gym shoes? A man after my own heart. I think I was falling in love.

He had a fresh haircut and I was getting seasick from all of the waves in his head. Oh, and he smelled good too. I had smoke coming out of my ears.

"So how long have you managed the restaurants?"

"Four years now."

"Did you study management in college?"

"No I didn't go to college." Okay, so college isn't for everyone. I can overlook that.

"Were you already working at one of the restaurants in high school?"

"Look, if you're trying to narrow down my age ranges then don't bother. All you have to do is ask." Damn. He didn't have to bust me out like that.

"So how old are you?"

"How old did you assume I was?"

"So you're mocking me. That's cute."

"No you're cute." Sarcasm will get you nowhere. But flattering, oh it'll take you places.

"I'm twenty-seven. And to answer your question, yes. I've been working at the Bayou Bistro since junior year in high school. After graduation I moved up to shift manager and eventually worked my way into general management by the age of twenty-five. That's about your age right?"

"If you want to know how old I am, all you have to do is ask."

"I just did." he replied. All right, so I wasn't as smooth as him. I dove back into the conversation quickly to avoid making an ass of myself.

"I'm twenty-three. Does that bother you?"

"Why would it? You're a woman aren't you?" All woman. Come here let me show you. Control yourself Rita.

"Indeed I am." This man had me so hot I had to go to the ladies room and freshen up. No matter how mature I was, my age showed itself sometimes. I hopped on the phone immediately and called my girlfriend Shawntee back home.

"What's up girl you would not believe this." I began. "Tell me why I am having breakfast with the finest man in New Orleans. Hell, possibly the finest man in the world."

"Who is he?" she replied.

"Can't give you full details right now but all I've got to say is white gold, diamond watch, linen pants suit, deep waves in hair, muscles and tank top. I'll give you details later. Love you. Bye."

I returned to the table cool, calm and collective. Our food was ready and he actually waited before chowing down.

"Is everything alright? I thought I was going to have to come in after you."

"Everything's fine. Ladies rooms are always crowded."

"We don't have that problem. We just aim, pee and shake it off." Did he just go there? I hope it's a little bit of washing of the hands included in that routine.

"So, Rita. I assume you're a college girl. Going to school here?"

"Actually no, I'm not a student. But I did study undergrad in California."

"LA?"

"Berkley."

"Impressive."

"Graduated top of my class. Summa cum Laude."

"You said you want a latte?" I'll let him slide on that one.

"No. It's a form of honors."

"So what are you in town for? Vacationing?" he asked.

"No, business. I'm a marketing manager for Candy Records in Chicago."

"Chicago. That's where you're from?"

"Born and raised."

We went on and on about Chicago and the music industry. I can talk about myself for hours. But I wanted to know more about him. After breakfast, we took a ferry ride on a small river. I wasn't too fond of the swamps. It was a little cool on the ferry and my nipples were like little buttons on my dress.

"You look a little cold. Here take my shirt." Yeah, I bet I looked cold. It was cool but I instantly heated up when he took off his shirt. His caramel complexion glistened in the sunlight. His muscles looked like caramel apples and I just wanted to take a bite.

"So what's on your agenda for today, Rita?" Normally I try not to be so available but there were a few exceptions to the rule; especially when you're this fine.

"Nothing particular."

"So I have you all to myself for the day?"

"For the day. I'm only here for three more days. My flight leaves out Saturday evening." Hint, Hint. He can have me for the weekend if he wants.

"Well I guess we'll have to make the best with what we've got. Tell you what, let me make the next three days a weekend you'll never forget."

"I can live with that." A weekend I'll never forget? My business trip just turned into a vacation.

"I was thinking maybe we can catch a movie this evening. And at dinner, I can tell you more about myself."

"That will be nice."

After the ferry ride, I retired to my room. While I bathed, I daydreamed of Jeff taking me on a fantastic voyage. Not a trip, you know, sexually. The phone rang and nearly startled me.

"Hello?"

"How's my favorite girl?" Jeff's voice was deep and relaxing. It damn there hypnotized me.

"I'm your favorite girl now? So you've just claimed me, huh?"

"Well, for as long as you will have me." I'll have you everyday if I can.

"How did you know where I lodged? I've been wondering that ever since I got the surprise."

"So I take it you like the watch." I had totally forgotten about the watch. My ungrateful ass never even thanked him.

"Do pardon my ignorance. I was so engulfed in the moment that I forgot to thank you. Such an expensive peace offering don't you think?"

"All the diamonds in the world couldn't buy that smile."

"But it's a start," I replied.

"Will you be ready soon? The movie starts at six."

"I'll be ready. Should I meet you at your place?"

"No. I'll pick you up at the hotel." Well, this gives me a chance to see how he's riding. Pretty nice, I assume. I'm sure running two restaurants pay pretty well. It's not like he has kids or anything. Or does he? I've been so busy talking about myself all day that I haven't had the chance to get down to the basics with him.

Jeff arrived around five-thirty and met me down in the lobby.

"You look nice, baby." Baby? We're moving on up the pet name ladder, aren't we?

"Thank you. Shall we?"

"We shall."

We exited on the sidewalk and Jeff proceeded down the street. After walking two blocks I just had to ask.

"Where's your car?"

"I left it at home. It's a nice night and the movie theatre is only a few blocks away. I thought it'd be romantic." Romantic? Tell my three-inch stilettos about romantic. My dogs were barking by the time we got to the theatre. I couldn't even stand in line for popcorn.

"Jeff, I'll meet you inside. I'm going to go find us some good seats." Jeff returned with a tub of popcorn. I'm not a popcorn eater. I should have asked for some gummy worms.

"Feet hurt?"

"How did you know?"

"I could tell by the way you limped into the theatre." He reached down and removed my pumps.

"What are you doing?"

"Put your feet up here," he said as he patted his lap. The theatre was rather empty so I guess it wouldn't hurt to get a little foot massage in public. His hands felt so good and so strong. I wanted to do him right then and there.

"Feel better?" Hell yeah. It even took a minute for me to register what he was saying.

"Yes. That was nice. But you didn't have to."

"Now what type of man would I be if I let my girl walk around with sore feet?" His girl? Okay so he wanted to live in this little fantasy relationship for a couple of days. That was cool. I didn't want to ruin the moment with dumb questions anyway.

The movie was over and we went down the street for dinner and drinks. The waiter greeted Jeff by name as if he was a regular.

"Come here often?"

"This is my favorite restaurant."

"I have a couple of questions I'd like to ask you. If that's okay with you."

"Trivia! Sure, I like questions."

"Do you have a girlfriend?"

"No."

"Why not? What's wrong with you?" He laughed at my gesture.

"Nothing. I'm just at a point in my life where I'm focused on my career and not women. Besides, no one as fine as you has stepped into my life in a long time." Fine? Who me? Hey!

"Any kids?" I continued.

"Nope. Maybe in the future, though. After I get married." At least we know he wants a future with someone.

"Go to church?"

"Every Sunday. I mentor the young men of the church." A God-fearing man too.

"So what do you like to do in your free time?" We had covered the basics. No girlfriend, no kids and a churchgoer. Why couldn't he live in Chicago?

Later that evening, we took a long stroll down to the swamp. The full moon shined bright above our heads. It was beautiful. Everything about this night, about him, seemed like a fairytale.

"Too bad I'll be leaving Saturday. Everything seems too good to be true."

"You don't have to leave. You can stay here." My laugh echoed across the swamp.

"And do what?"

"Nothing. I'll take care of you."

"That's sweet. But Saturday night, when I step off that plane, I step back into reality. And baby boy…you ain't in it."

We both laughed and went on about our goals and ambitions. It was well after midnight before we decided to head home.

"I think we've had enough for one night." I didn't want to go home. Although I was extremely tired, I just wanted to lie in his arms and fly away.

We approached the stoop and Jeff leaned in for a hug. I shrugged as if I was insulted.

"You can't walk your girl to her door?" I ask flirtingly.

"Well I didn't want to overstep my boundaries." He walked me upstairs to my door and I invited him in. We decided to order a movie and enjoy each other's company a little while longer.

As we lie there on the bed, I couldn't help but think about kissing him. The feeling must have been mutual because he looked up and noticed me gazing at him. Jeff pulled me close and I got goose bumps as my body slid in towards his. His cologne smelled so good and his skin was soft like cotton candy.

Was I tripping' or was I just extremely caught up in the moment. I acted as if I was really into the movie to keep my attention off his muscles.

"Do you mind if I use your restroom?"

"By all means."

Once he entered the restroom, I repositioned myself. I was a bit uncomfortable lying on my belly while trying to watch TV. I propped a pillow between my back and the headboard and stretched my legs a little. That's more like it.

When Jeff walked out of the restroom, I noticed that he had removed his shirt. Ooh, a black tank top this time. I waited for him to join me on the other side of the bed to continue the movie but he didn't. He crawled up onto the bed from the bottom up, right on top of me. He lifted my chin with his index finger and we indulged in the longest, sweetest, most sexual kiss ever. Umm, Umm, Umm.

What I was about to do next was well thought out in case something like this were to happen. I fumbled a little with his belt buckle and, uh……….need I say more? Of course. Jeff noticed that I was having a little trouble so he helped me out a little.

While he undid his pants, I clicked the tube with the remote control. I watched in amazement as he relit the candles that were already set from the night before. Wonder if he had pre-planned too? The black boxer briefs accentuated his tight ass and muscular legs. I didn't bother to undress. I wanted him to do it for me. And I must admit he did a great job. We engaged in the most drawn out sexual act ever. It felt so good and so right that it just had to be wrong. And it was.

Here I was having the craziest sex ever with a perfect stranger. Someone whom I'd probably never see again in my life. Honestly? Can't say that I feel guilty about it. Men do it all of the time. As long as I'm protecting myself, I'm cool. I'm not going back to Chicago with any little bastard babies or cooties. So for the next two days: I'm getting down with the get down.

I rolled over the next day to a cold pillow and a note that read, "Didn't want to wake you, angel, but I have to get to work. Come down to the restaurant when you get hungry." I did just that. It was already past noon and I had slept through my morning workout and breakfast. I felt a little hung over from the sex so I ended up dipping in and out of the restaurant briefly.

At lunch, I told Jeff that I had to have a talk with him. Kind of a scary thing to say the day after sex, huh? I was leaving the next day and I wanted my last rendezvous to be spectacular. Let's face it; if it's going to be all about sex, it might as well be good sex. I wanted this experience to be one that I'll never forget.

The phone rang and I knew that Jeff was anxious to find out what was up.

"Hello?"

"Hey, kitten. What's up? What did you want to talk to me about?"

"Well, Jeff. I don't know how to say this but…."

"Man, the sex was that bad?" He said in a soft tone.

"No, not at all. It was great. That's what I wanted to talk to you about, actually. Since this will be our last night together, I wanted it to be special."

"What did you have in mind?"

"I'll leave that up to you. Just be creative."

"That's cool. But who said that this would be our last night together. How did you know if I wasn't coming to see you in Chicago or not?"

"I didn't. Why would you do a thing like that?"

"Damn. I could have sworn you were my girl?" Okay, okay. This relationship fantasy has gotten a little out of control. What can I say to this man to keep tonight pleasant and not mislead him?

"Of course, sweetie. I was just testing you." Come on Rita. Are you crazy or what? How could I go along with something as bizarre as that?

"Tell you what," he started. "Meet me at the swamp at nine o'clock tonight."

"The swamp?"

"You remember. The little river where we took the ferry ride."

"Okay sweetie. See you at the restaurant for dinner?"

"No, not tonight. I've got some business to take care of."

"Oh, okay. See you at nine." Guess I'll be dining alone then.

I spent most of my day packing my things for my flight out tomorrow. I had a great time in New Orleans but I was ready to get my black ass back to Chicago. My next conference wasn't for another month, so that gives me a little time to chill at home. I decided to call my family and friends and inform them of my arrival tomorrow night.

"Hey mom, it's me, Rita."

"I know who you are, nut. What's up baby girl? How was your trip?"

"Fantastic. I'll be heading back in tomorrow night."

"Around what time?"

"I should be stepping off of the plane around ten twenty. How's pop?"

"Pop is pop. You know how that goes. He's in the room bitching at the TV right now."

"Tell him I said, hey."

"I'll tell him later. I don't feel like talking to him right now." My parents were a riot. Always fussing and complaining. You'd think after 30 years of marriage, they'd just shut-up! They argue and complain, and neither one of them ever has a point.

"Well I'm going to go mom. I just wanted to let you know that I'll be home tomorrow."

"Okay baby, call me when you get home."

It was good to hear my mom's voice. Even when I'm at home I barely get to see her. It's like I always have something to do. People always tell me to spend more time with my parents. They're not going to be around one day.

I dialed my girlfriend Shawntee but she wasn't there. Here voicemail picked up saying, "Hi you have reached Shawntee's line, I'm not in at the moment, do leave a message after the beep."

"Hey girl it's me, Rita. Just called to tell you that I'll be home tomorrow night. I'll give you a call when I get in. Love ya'. Bye."

Shawntee was my best friend in the world. We grew up together and the only time we've ever been separated was while I was in college. Shawntee's four years older than me but it's hard to tell. I have an old soul so I relate to everyone. Shawntee has twin daughter's that just turned six. I really hate I missed their birthday because I'm their godmother. I did get to send them birthday souvenirs from New Orleans that they loved.

It's kind of tough being twenty-three and being away from home all of the time. Your family's your support and even though, mine isn't as supportive, I still miss them. I'm the first in my family to graduate college and do something with myself. My older sister was on that path until she was killed in a car accident ten years ago. I really miss her a lot. I look at her pictures often to remind me of all the dreams and plans she had for us. She used to always talk about being a dancer and going to New York to study performing arts. At the age of fifteen, she was run over by a drunk driver. She was coming from a convenience store when the car flew up onto the curb and landed on the sidewalk. I can still picture the splattered gallon of milk and blood streaming down the curb into the sewer. It took my family years to overcome that loss. My dad hasn't been right since.

I miss her dearly and sometimes dream of us playing double-Dutch again. She loved to sing as her high-pitched voice rang up the block.

"Two, four, six, eight, ten. Two one o, two o, three o, four o, five o, six o…"

Tears start to roll down my face and I felt myself getting weak. I laid down for a nap only to dream of my sister Sarah a little more.

When I awoke from my nap, I realized I had overslept and it was already nine o'clock. I wonder why Jeff hasn't called me? A brief shower, quick brush, spray of perfume and I was out the door. I caught a cab over to the lake. As I exited the cab I noticed a glow on the opposite side of the lake deep within the trees. I didn't know what it was and wasn't trying to find out. It was too damn creepy for me.

A large figure emerged from the glow and I realized it was Jeff.

"Walk around to this side," he yelled from afar. His voice echoed in the trees and I wondered if anyone else could hear us. I was excited to see what Jeff had in store for us. I finally made it to the other side and was amazed at the site.

Candles were everywhere surrounding a white blanket covered with rose petals and chocolates. There were two pillows and a radio nearby that played soft jazz. It was like a flight of the imagination. Everything was so unbelievable that I had to pinch myself.

"Champagne my lady?" Jeff handed me a chilled glass of champagne and we made a toast.

"To new beginnings." What in the hell is he talking about? Oh well, who cares. I'm about to get me some.

"To new beginnings." I guzzled down my drink and flopped down on the blanket. Jeff immediately retrieved me from the blanket.

"May I have this dance?" He wants to dance too. This man went all out. I can learn to like this. We danced for a while and then my stomach made the loudest roar I had ever heard.

"I'm sorry. I'm a little hungry."

"I thought you might be." He went behind a bush and returned with a picnic basket.

"I prepared us a little late night snack." In the basket were fruit, chips, and a couple of finger sandwiches.

"You've really outdone yourself Mr. Bridges. I'm impressed."

"There's more where that came from," he replied. I didn't know what the heck he was talking about and didn't care. All I knew is that I was in heaven.

Jeff started kissing the small of my back as I lied there on my stomach. As he trailed them to the back of my neck, he rolled me over and we engaged in another one of those whammies. I could not believe what was happening. He wanted to get down right there in the woods. My body quivered as he held me close.

"Relax," he started. "Just relax and let me take control." Yes sir! All aboard. The funny thing is that I wasn't even scared. Being spotted by someone was the least of my concerns. It was the perfect night for a time like this. We can clearly see the moon and stars from where we were.

"Too bad I'm leaving tomorrow."

"Too bad I can't come with you."

"There's nothing in Chicago. You're not missing anything."

"Yes I am. You. I'm missing you already Rita."

"If you like, you can stay the night with me back at the hotel."

"I'd love that. But that's not enough. I want to stay like this forever."

"Yeah, Yeah. Then Monday comes, and we both go back to our boring jobs and we'll forget all about each other." I noticed he wasn't laughing with me.

"Rita I was serious when I called you my girl. Now I know that a long distance relationship is going to be hard at first, but we'll both get the hang of it." This man was actually serious. How in the hell did he think this was going to work with us being miles and miles away? I like him and all, but I hadn't considered being with him seriously.

How could I? My life is too busy. I have no time for a boyfriend. Not even one that I don't have to see everyday.

"How is this supposed to work, Jeff. We'll never get a chance to see each other."

"Yes we will. I'll come to Chicago some weekends, and you can come here some weekends." His teary eyes convinced me that he had put a lot of thought into this and I truly did not want to disappoint him. So I did what any sane woman would do.

"Okay baby. We'll give it a shot. You're right. I can come see you and you the same." What? Yeah right. Like I was going to put him down right there: while I'm miles and miles away from home, away from friends and family, in the middle of the woods. Huh! I'll let him down easy once I get back home. Besides, I didn't want to ruin such a good night, anyway.

Back at the hotel, I realized that I was no longer wrapped up in the moment. I was ready to flee this sex prison and get back to my normal life. Jeff was beginning to give me the creeps. We ended up spending the rest of our night discussing a false future together. We talked about careers, homes, even kids. This man was nuts. It was like he was desperate for a relationship. I was just down right horny. That's it!

I was praying that he wouldn't be there the next morning. Unfortunately there was no note and no cold pillow. Instead, Jeff was embedded into the pillow with his mouth wide opened and a drool stain below it. He looked mighty comfortable as he snored loudly and farted in his sleep. I tried to creep out of bed but he pulled me right back in.

"Where you think you're going?"

"I have to go to the bathroom."

"Don't take too long," he said as he slapped me across my bottom. What the hell?

Is it me or is this cat extremely too relaxed? I felt that it would be safer to shower while I was already in the restroom. Something tells me that he wants to be posted for a while. That something was right.

"Jeff, baby. Don't you have to work today?"

"Nope. I took off today. My shift managers can handle it without me. So we have the whole day. I think we'll order room service and movies today." I was right. I did not plan on being laid up in my room all day. It was my last few hours being in New Orleans.

"I figured you've seen enough of New Orleans this week. I thought it would be nice just to relax with your man today."

"Is that what you thought?" I could sense that he didn't appreciate my sarcasm.

So there we were. Eating, sleeping, screwing and shitting our whole day away. I was glad when six o'clock hit. I was packed, dressed and headed towards the airport. I was prepared to give him a dramatic goodbye outside the lobby, but Jeff jumped right into my cab.

"What are you doing?"

"I'm riding with my baby to make sure she gets on th[e plane]. Great. Just what I need. A heightened dramatic scene. [It's] a half-an-hour to the airport. After checking in, I ca[n see he's] getting a little hazy. He looked as if he had that little lump in [his throat.] You know the one you get when you're trying not to cry. Oh please. Give me a break. It's only been three days. It took God longer than that to create the world. So how in Pete's sake did he create a relationship that fast?

"Give me a hug sweetie I've got to go." He gave me a tight hug, a long kiss, and another tight ass hug.

"Okay, Jeff, I got to go," I said as I pried him off of me.

"Call me as soon as you get home, Rita."

"Okay, bye." I was halfway to the terminal when I heard his voice.

"Rita." I turned around and went back to see what he wanted now.

"I just wanted to tell you that this has been the best three days in my life and that I've fallen in love with you." Hold up, wait a minute. Did he just say what I thought he said? Yes, the hell, he did. Sadly, he paused as if he wanted me to say it back.

"Okay. Thanks."

"Thanks? That's it?"

"I'll call you when I get home." I rushed back to the terminal to escape the tears that rolled down Jeff's face. I didn't know what to tell him. I felt so bad that I had misled this man. I like him, but this would never work out. I don't even know enough about this man to make such a decision.

The company had a limo pick me up at the airport. This was great because I was tired of taking cabs. When I returned to my condo, I sat in my rocking chair on the balcony that overlooked the lake. Chicago's skyline never looked more beautiful to me. I sipped an apple martini while I checked my messages and called to check in with my family. I was most anxious to call Shawntee and tell her all about my little fling.

I was fast asleep when my phone rang through the apartment. I gazed at the clock before answering the phone. It was well after two in the morning. Who would be calling at this hour?

"Hello?"

"I thought I told you to call me when you got home?" Why did I even give this man my real number? I should have just ditched him completely.

"I'm sorry sweetie. I was so tired after I called my family that I just passed out." I couldn't believe what I was hearing. Did I just explain myself to this man? Was I crazy?

"So how was your flight?"

"Look, baby. I'm dead tired and I want to make it to church on time tomorrow, so I'm going to have to go."

"If you must." Did I sense some hostility in his voice? I think I did.

"I must. I'll talk to you later. Bye?" This man was out of his rabbit ass mind calling me at that hour. I had it in me to curse his ass out. I rolled over and buried myself back into my white, fluffy, down covers.

The following morning I awoke to a loud, obnoxious ringing in my ear. The telephone rang through my ears like church bells at noon. I should have known that it was Jeff. It had become apparent that this man was a nut case. I didn't bother to answer. Luckily he lived miles away, so avoiding him would be easy.

It felt good to be home. I was almost an hour late for service, but the choir was still singing and the sermon had not been delivered. I spotted my mom at the front row: largest hat to the right. My dad sat at the pew directly across from her. Sweat beaded up on his baldhead as he patted it with a handkerchief. I grew up in a small, storefront church where most of the members were originally from the south. They engaged in extended devotion services singing long, drawn-out "Dr. Watts" from the slavery days.

The pastor begins his sermon with song, "I love the Lord, He heard my cry..."

Why do these ministers insist on putting you to sleep before they deliver the sermon? After service I tipped-toed behind my parents and surprised them with a big hug and kiss.

"Hey ma, hey pa."

"Rita! Oh come here, baby. I missed you so much." It was obvious that my mom was ecstatic. My dad always showed few emotions, but I knew that he was glad to see me.

"Hi daddy."

"Hey baby girl. Welcome home. How was your trip?" I proceeded to tell them all about the trip but was constantly interrupted by church members who were welcoming me home.

My parents and I went over to my aunt's house for a barbecue. My family always gathered for dinner on Sundays. My return made this dinner a special one. It was nice to be around family. As long as I was home, I tried my best to spend time with the ones I loved. It was hard to ignore the constant vibrating on my hip from my cell phone. Most calls were from colleagues, but the majority of the calls were from Jeff.

I called him that night before turning in. I knew that the next morning, I would be tied up in meetings, conferences and phone calls. Jeff and I talked for a while about Chicago and what it has to offer. He seemed extremely interested in the workforce and tourists attractions.

"Man, Jeff. You act as if you want to move to Chicago. What's up with that?"

"Maybe I do. I wasn't kidding when I said I loved you, Rita. I know it seems crazy but that's the funny thing about love. It happens when you least expect it. You may not feel the same way about me but.... If you just give me a chance I can prove that I'm the man for you. We were meant to be together."

He sounded bizarre and sincere at the same time. He was fine and he did have potential. I just wasn't ready for anything serious. I didn't think that I was up for the challenge.

"Jeff, you have to understand that I'm not as available when I'm at home. I have to get up and go into the office everyday just like everyone else. I also travel a lot. We'll never be able to see each other and I'll constantly have to leave you. Is that the life that you want to live?"

"If I'm living it with you, yes!"

"Well we'll see. For what it's worth, I'll give it a try. I love you. Just trust that."

Trust was a very critical word for me. I didn't trust anyone but my parents. I've seen where trust can take you and I didn't want to go there. No matter how sincere he sounded, I still had my doubts. I do respect his honesty and I like that fact that a successful, young woman like me didn't intimidate him. This would was normally the dead end to all of my relationships.

I can't say that I was glad to return to the office Monday morning. My desk was swamped with memos, post-its and schedules. Work, work, work. That's all I do. It was almost like I never left. My boss greeted me with a mid-conversation that didn't make any sense.

"So on the 29th you'll be headed to Los Angeles for two weeks and then over to Nevada. We've got a lot of territory to cover kiddo. So tighten up your presentation."

"Good morning Nick. Good to see you to. And by the way, what in the heck are you talking about?"

"Sorry, Rita. Welcome back, good to see you, all that good stuff. Everything that we just discussed is highlighted in this portfolio. After you review it, get back to me and let me know your approach on the situation. I'll see you tomorrow."

"See you tomorrow? The day just started. Where do you have to go?"

"To play golf. Duh!"

My boss had to be the coolest ever. I had a lot of freedom because I was sort of his star. I led the way to all contract negotiations. Bottom line; I made him a lot of money. As a result of this, he looked out for me. Normally I would spend a day or two preparing my proposals and presentations. My personal secretary monitored all appointments, schedules, meetings and travel. She sometimes took the initiative and power-pointed my notes and presentations for me. This saved me a lot of time and allowed me to chill the remainder of the week. I surprised Jeff with a phone call around lunchtime.

"Jeff Bridges, please?"

"Jeff's not in this week. He's on vacation. Would you like to speak to the acting manager?" The young woman replied.

"Oh, no thank you. I'll try his cell."

On vacation. He didn't say anything about going on vacation. What in the world was going on? I wasn't sure but I was certainly going to find out. I called Jeff's cell phone and there was no answer.

"Hey sweetie this is Rita. I called you at work and they said that you were on vacation. Give me a call back to let me know what's going on. Talk to you later. Bye."

Oh well. I guess I'll just wait until he calls back. I decided to actually do some work, to keep my mind off of Jeff. For someone who didn't want to be with this man, I sure was concerned. I guess I'm starting to develop feelings for him.

The warm breeze blowing into my office building relaxed me. I found myself drifting into a deep sleep. I told my secretary to hold my calls and I laid down on the leather sofa in my office. I was still a little tired from the trip due to the fact that Jeff and I had stayed up late the last few days. I dozed off as the summer breeze swept across my face.

"Rita," my intercom blurted out of nowhere. I damn there pissed myself. I wiped the slobber from the corners of my mouth and responded to the person on the other end.

"Yes."

"There's a gentleman here to see you."

"Who is it?"

"He says his name is Jeff Bridges." Jeff Bridges? Was this some sort of joke? I figured it was so I told the secretary to send him in. My clothes were a little disheveled and I didn't bother fixing them. I figured it was Shawntee playing a trick on me. She didn't work far away and she would often stop by on her lunch.

The doors opened and in walked the most handsome man to come into my life. It was Jeff. What in the hell? Was I still sleeping? It took me a minute to regain my composure. I was just sitting there with my mouth opened.

"Surprise baby. I told you I was coming to see you." Yeah but it's only been two days. What? When? How? I was at a lost for words.

"Damn baby. Aren't you glad to see me?" he asked.

"Hey you. What are you doing here?" I tried to sound sweet instead of frightened.

"That night after you left, I just didn't know what to do with myself. I missed you so much and longed to be in your presence." Longed to be in my presence? Was this cat for real?

"I just had to see you. So I thought I'd surprise you. Once you said that you would give us a try, I called my boss and told him that I was leaving town on a family emergency."

"So you just upped and got on a plane? This is wild. I just called you a few hours ago and they told me that you were on vacation. I just thought that maybe you had gotten sick or something."

"I saw your calls on my cell but I didn't want to ruin the surprise. These are for you." He extended his arm and handed me a bunch of purple tulips. They were my favorite. I'm surprised he remembered. I could hear a crowd gathering outside my office door. Everyone was eager to know who this handsome gentleman was. I never had male visitors on the job and everyone knew that I was man-less. I was blown away by such a surprise. This had to be one of the most shocking things to happen to me in a long time.

"So how long are you here for?"

"Four days and three nights. Is it okay if I stay with you?"

"Sure. Why not?" I could use a little more of that good loving that he put on me back in New Orleans. He would have been shit out of luck if I had left town again. Who leaves town and doesn't make reservations for lodging? He was definitely a risk taker.

I left work early and Jeff and I went back to my place. He wanted to take in his luggage and shower before we hit the streets. His jaws dropped in amazement as he entered the corridor.

"Your salary pays for all this?"

"It's a company owned condominium. I just pay utilities."

"And the beamer?"

"Company. I just fill the tank."

"Hum. Must be nice."

"It is."

I made a couple of calls while Jeff showered. He walked out butt ass naked and my temperature rose ten degrees. I guess he was reading my mind because he pounced on me while I was lying on the bed.

"I miss you so much," he started.

"I've been waiting on this for two days now."

We engaged in another one of our explicit sexual acts and returned to the showers: together this time. I dressed in a white short set and flat sandals that were appropriate for walking. We spent our day at Navy Pier for lunch, shopping and sightseeing. We ended the night with a horse and carriage ride across Grant Park. It was the perfect evening for romance.

"There are so many things for you to see in Chicago, Jeff. I can't wait to show you. We'll try to see as much as possible over the next three days. Did you enjoy yourself?"

"Of course I did. There's no rush. Whatever I don't get to see this trip, I'll see the next. This marks the beginning of a beautiful relationship." We raised our glasses in a toast and ended it with a sweet and gentle kiss.

Back at my place, we lamped on the patio and gazed at the skyline. We sipped zinfandel until our lips were numb and our tongues were tied. This made us more adventurous and pumped to do the unexpected. We made love right there on the patio. No blankets, no nothing. I'm sure half the people riding Lake Shore Drive saw us that night. I didn't even care. I was being spontaneous and loving it.

The next morning I awoke to the smell of waffles and sausage. Jeff was in the kitchen, my kitchen, fixing breakfast. He walked into the room wearing nothing but his underwear. You can see his third leg hanging below his boxers. The man was definitely well endowed. But that's not why I was with him. Is it? No, no. He's sweet, caring, sincere and daring. Jeff knew how to treat a lady and I could definitely learn to appreciate that.

Breakfast was delicious and the sex afterwards wasn't bad either. We were like dogs in heat. We humped before and after every meal and in the oddest places, too. Let's just say that you wouldn't want to eat on my kitchen table. You probably wouldn't want to sit on the sofa, take a shower or chill on the patio either. We even did it downstairs in the laundry room.

I'm sure by now that we've been spotted by some of my neighbors. We didn't get any complaints though. You should see some of the things that go on in these high-rises. Next time you're trailing the lakefront, take a pair of binoculars. This should keep you entertained for a while. I emailed my portfolio to Nick and took off the next few days. Jeff and I had a ball, and he decided to stay through the weekend.

I hated to see him go. I enjoyed his company and couldn't live without the sex. I drove him to Midway Airport and we had lunch before he boarded the plane. I could feel my eyes tearing up, but I didn't want to make a scene. It was almost like a fairy tale except it was reality. I was actually falling for this man. Jeff pulled me close and gave me a long, soft kiss.

"I'll see you soon baby."

"How soon?" Okay. He had me. I was right where he wanted me to be. I was actually missing him already.

"Don't worry baby. I have a few more weeks' vacation and a couple of other benefit days. It'll be soon. We'll talk everyday until then."

"Promise?"

"I promise."

This man had me whipped. I couldn't let go of the fact that I had fallen for this man. Was this love or lust? Who knows? All I know is that I was happy. I wanted this feeling to last forever. When I stepped into my cold, empty apartment, I realized what was missing. My man.

2
BUNDLES OF JOY

Weeks had passed and Jeff and I were growing closer and closer. He even came to see me while I was on a business trip in California. I showed him the old campus and a few of my former professors entertained him with stories of my college life. He was learning more about me but there was still a gap in his past. I didn't know what it was but it pondered my mind. Jeff was too good to be true and I knew that he had some skeletons in his closet that would soon reveal them.

Summer was almost over and I had an open schedule for a couple of weeks so I decided to surprise Jeff. I stepped into his restaurant and asked the host to retrieve him from the back. He returned with the blankest look that I had ever seen. It was almost like it was bad timing.

"Surprise, baby. Aren't you glad to see me?"

"Uh. Yeah. What are you doing here?"

"I took a vacation and decided to come and surprise you. Was that a bad idea?"

"No, not at all. I'm glad to see you, baby. Come on back into my office."

I followed Jeff to his small, secluded office in the back of the restaurant. It was almost like it was a separate building or an annex. He closed the door and next thing I knew, we were all over the desk.

It had been almost a month and a half since we last made love. I was looking good, he was looking good, and we both were hot. When we were done christening his office, he said that he had a surprise for me. He pulled a small box from his safe and got down on one knee.

"Rita, I have never met anyone like you before. I am so happy that God turned my guardian angel into a human. I can't think of a better time to ask you this. Will you marry me?"

The box opened and platinum, three-carat diamond almost blinded me. Is this for real? Couldn't be. But…

"You didn't even know that I was coming. How did you? Why did you?"

I was at a lost for words. Nothing like this had ever happened to me before. I was stuck between a rock and a hard place. What was I to say? My heart said wait and think about it, but my mouth said,

"Yes."

"Yes?"

"Yes. But how will this work. I can't leave my job and skip town."

"No, but I can. I'll give my boss a notice and I'm sure he'll let me stay until I find something in Chicago. It's a big city. There should be plenty of opportunities."

"Well there are certainly plenty of restaurants. Oh my God," I screeched. "I can't believe this."

As excited as I was, I couldn't help but think of what my parents were going to say. They didn't take care of me, but I still valued their opinions. This was going to start a lot of turmoil back in Chicago. I could just feel it. Who cares? I was happy and fed up with being alone. I wanted a husband.

While vacationing, I realized that I had never seen Jeff's place. I had reserved a room for us and never once thought about crashing at his place. I'm sure the room was more romantic, but I still wanted to see how he lived.

"Jeff, when will I get to see your place? I know you want to show it off one last time before you start packing."

"I don't know baby. It's no where near as nice as your place and about one third the size."

"That's okay with me. I'd probably be staying with my parents if it weren't for the company. I still want to see it. Let's go. Now. Please?"

"Okay, but my boy is staying with me for a while. He and his wife are having problems and I told him that he could crash there for a while. Let me just call and make sure he isn't walking around in his drawls."

I waited while Jeff went in the lobby of the hotel to call his friend. I couldn't understand why he just didn't use his cell phone. Maybe he was almost out of minutes. He returned shortly and we headed off to see his house.

"So this is your car, huh?" It was my first time riding in Jeff's car.

"It's not luxury but it gets me to where I have to go."

"Who has a baby?"

"Huh?" he replied.

"I can see the imprint from the car seat in the back. Who has a kid?"

"Oh. My sister borrows my car from time to time. She has a little boy. Two years old. I hadn't even noticed that it left a print."

"A nephew, huh? I assume I'm meeting the family before I skip town?"

"Honestly baby." he began with a solemn tone.

"I really don't mess with my family like that. They're too nosy and I don't like going around them. They keep up too much mess. I'd rather keep you all to myself."

Jeff's story sounded a little flaky, but I know how some families can be. I was lucky enough to have a not-so-functional family. Finally we arrived to Jeff's home. It wasn't exactly what I expected, but then again, I haven't seen the homes of many bachelors'. I expected it to be messy, but the small, framed house was actually pretty clean. The white, painted porch with the swing was a classic. You certainly won't see one like this in Chicago.

I noticed that there weren't many brick homes in the area. The neighborhood was bombarded with bi-level shacks. I was impressed on the inside. I noticed the details as I pranced across his polished, hardwood floors. Everything was so plain, so black and white. Of course he had the standard, black, leather three-piece living room set that all cheap, bachelors get. Everything else sort of blended in; the cheap, black, entertainment center, the black bedroom set, black appliances and the infamous black oriental area rug.

He even had the three, black oriental paper fans on the wall to compliment the rug: The touch of a tacky ex-girlfriend. Whoever she was, her name was written all over the walls. And the floor for that matter.

"So are you ready to go?" Damn. He was mighty eager to get me out of there.

"Are you in a hurry?" I asked.

"No, there's just nothing here to do and I figured we'd go out. You know, catch a bite to eat or something."

Bullshit ain't about nothing! I don't know what Jeff was up to but I wasn't having it.

""No. We should stay in. I think I'll stay here tonight. What do you have in the fridge? You can cook for me. Doesn't that sound romantic?"

"I'm not a very good cook."

"I'll be the judge of that," I replied.

"There's no food in the house."

"We can go to the market."

I don't know what it was that he was trying to pull but he could give it up. I was staying and that was that. Besides, it gave me a taste of what he's like living with.

Around dinnertime I could tell that Jeff didn't know his way around the kitchen. He seemed a little disheveled and didn't know where anything was.

"Here. Let me help you," I offered.

"You act as if you don't know where anything is. This is your house, isn't it?"

"Yes. I just don't cook."

"Yeah, but you should at least know where the dishes are."

I could tell that Jeff was a bit disturbed, so I decided to take over in the kitchen. He watched the sports channel while I whipped up one of my down-home specialties; smothered pork chops, rice, peas and buttermilk biscuits. We topped the dinner off with candlelight and cheap wine.

Jeff ate like he had never eaten before. He sopped his plate and licked his fingers. His mouth was all greasy and he still had nerves to lean in for a kiss.

"This was the best meal I'd ever had. You've really outdone yourself, baby. Thank you."

"You're welcome. I guess. There's more where that came from. Got room for dessert?"

"Dessert?" he yelled. "You bake, too? Oh hell yeah! I'm going to enjoy being married to you."

His eyes widened as I bought out the key lime pie, topped with whip cream and sprinkled with graham cracker crumbs.

"This pie looks like it needs to be on display at a bake shop. And it's good, too," he said as whip cream flew out of his mouth.

As messy as he looked, he was still fine. And to think, he was soon to be all mine. I gazed at my ring while Jeff devoured the pie. I couldn't help but think of everyone's gripes when I got back home. No one was going to believe this. Correction. No one would want to believe this.

"Should I tell my parents immediately, or should I wait until you move to Chicago before I tell them?" I asked.

"I think you should tell them immediately. Get them prepared for my arrival. I don't want to walk into any family feuds."

Why not? He had started it. He had some nerves, sending me into the line of fire like that. I really didn't appreciate his response. I'd hate to think that the man that I was about to marry was a wimp.

The night was long and I hadn't gone back to the hotel for my clothes, so I wore one of his oversized t-shirts. I must have looked hot in it because it led to an unbelievable night of lovemaking. Hell, I could be wearing a snowsuit with sandals and a bonnet, playing a ukulele and it'll still end up a passionate night. It didn't matter to Jeff. His stamina was that of an iron horse. Making kids would definitely not be a problem in future.

Upon my return to Chicago, I set Jeff up with a few prospective employers. I was eager to get him home. Home. That sounded nice. The thought of coming home everyday to my man was a fine one. We would work all day and screw all night. Who said being single was the good life? I was soon to prove them wrong.

I made the big announcement to my parents as soon as I returned. My mom was devastated. She cried and cursed and damn there passed out. My dad on the other hand was a little more reserved. He slowly walked down to the basement and shortly after he returned polishing his rifle.

"So when do we meet him?"

"Come on daddy. He's not a bad guy."

"But you barely even know him. What if he's wanted for murder or something?" my mom screeched.

"He's not. You're being a bit far-fetched."

"Oh there she goes using those fancy words again," mumbled my dad.

I spent the whole night convincing my parents that Jeff was the man for me. They wanted to believe that he was just after my money. Bottom line, he was about to be my husband and that was that.

"It's not like he has to live or sleep here. I'm a grown woman and I make my own decisions. Jeff will be my husband and as far as I'm concerned, this conversation is over."

My dad scowled and my mom started calling on the Lord. She swore that if he did wrong by me that she would have nothing to do with it.

"I don't want to hear it," she said. "You'll see. You'll see. Oh Lord when will she ever learn?"

My mom always has been an overeater. I was determined to prove to them that Jeff was the man for me, no matter what. The only person who knew what was right for Rita was Rita. Jeff would be a part of my life very soon and I had some preparations to make. First thing first, I called all of my "boys" and announced that I was engaged and couldn't date them anymore. This was to avoid any drama in the near future. Then I hid all of the pictures and videotapes that I never wanted Jeff to see. College was wild and I still had all of the memorabilia to glance at.

I wondered if Jeff was doing some of the same things. I would hope that he wouldn't bring photos of his past to Chicago. Trust me, if his past was half as wild as mine was, I didn't want to see it. The key is to stay together, not grow apart. Jeff and I had taken some pictures on his last visit to Chicago, so I replaced all of my pictures in the frames with pictures of he and I.

Married. Mrs. Rita Bridges. That sounded nice. Everyone at the office is not going to believe this one. I told my boss first thing Monday morning and he congratulated me. He also announced that he had a surprise for me.

"The company banquet is in a month. Do you think that your fiancé will be in town by then?" he asked.

"Hopefully. Why?"

"I have a big announcement to make and I think he'd love to be there for it."

I don't know what my boss was up to but I'm sure I'd like it. There are always new incentives and perks offered to us on the job. He's probably giving out bonuses. I could use one. Jeff will probably want to add his own touch to the apartment when he gets here. We'll be able to do a little shopping before he starts work.

Later in the week I received a dozen roses at my office. They were from Jeff. The note read,

"Thanks for the job leads. See you sooner than you think."

I didn't know how soon but I was definitely excited to see him. This new lifestyle was going to be fun. I hated being alone and I was well overdue for some permanent company. Oh, casual sex, too. That night, I walked around my apartment and took one last look at it. Pretty soon, it won't be so cold and quiet. I had prepared a relaxing evening with a warm bubble bath and chilled champagne. The buzzer rang out loudly just as I put my toes in the water.

Who in the hell could this be? I wasn't expecting any company. As I walked to the door, I couldn't help but think that it was someone I had previously dated that just couldn't take no for an answer. I really was not up for a drama scene.

"Who is it?" I yelled into the intercom.

"Honey I'm home." a voice rang out.

It was Jeff. I threw on my robe and ran downstairs to meet him. Parked in the driveway behind him was a moving van. I assumed he had ditched the shoddy furniture and just bought his most valuable possessions. God bless him. The bellhop carried the luggage to the elevator and help Jeff settle in. Jeff raised his nose in the air and took a long whiff.

"Bubble bath? I came just in time."

We didn't waste anytime. As we sat in the hot tub, we discussed all of our plans. Jeff informed me that he had three interviews scheduled for the next week. I couldn't believe that this was really happening: and so fast at that.

"How did you leave so soon? What about your house?"

"Well, I decided to rent my house to my boy for the time being. If he and his wife decide to get back together then I'll just put it on the market."

"So what now?"

"We interview and we wait. Until then, we get busy."

One thing I loved about Jeff was his sense of humor. He was always comical. Jeff was just what I needed; funny, cute, smart. He was every woman's dream. I felt so lucky to have him in my life.

We spent the weekend shopping and dining. By the looks of Jeff's light travel, it was apparent that Jeff needed new clothes. We were able to catch a few specials at some of the department stores. Our biggest problem was shoes. Jeff couldn't understand why he couldn't sport the country style in the big city.

"Baby. You can't wear lime green gators to an interview."

"It'll match the white suit that we just bought. I can even wear a lime green hanky in the pocket. I'll look smooth, baby."

Okay, okay. So Mr. Perfect had some flaws. So what. There's always room for improvement. I convinced him to get a nice pair of shoes that seemed nearly colorless to him. They were interview appropriate.

When the time came, it was Jeff's turn to work his magic. He looked good, smelled good, and was ready to take on the big city. I can't say that I was concerned. Jeff was a big boy. People liked him. Especially women. He was a charmer. Unfortunately, there is always that one who could care less about your charming good looks. By the end of the week, we were down on our luck. No one had hired Jeff and he was beginning to worry.

"I don't know, baby," he began. "Maybe I should have just stayed in Louisiana until I had something etched in stone. I was just so frantic to be with you. I wasn't thinking logically."

"Don't worry sweetie. Something will come. It's only been a week. Give it some time."

"It's just a little more competitive here in the big city. I have to step up my game."

Jeff was discouraged and there was nothing that I could say to help. I prayed and I knew that it was only a matter of time before Jeff would find a job in Chicago. My prayers were answered sooner than I thought. Jeff called me at my office and announced the good news.

"So when do you start?" I asked.

"He wants me to come back tomorrow morning."

"This is great, honey."

"Yeah. I hear Palagios' is a very prestigious restaurant."

"It is. My girlfriend and I dine there often. I'm so happy for you."

"We're celebrating tonight. Put that little red number on with the red pumps."

"Okay sweetie. See you later. Love you. Bye."

"I love you, too. Bye."

Shortly after my conversation with Jeff, my girlfriend, Shawntee, called me. I was happy to hear from her. I haven't had much time for girl talk since the engagement.

"Hey girl, what's up?"

"Hey my ass. What happened to you? You were supposed to call me back like two weeks ago."

"I know. I'm sorry. A lot's been happening since then."

"You bet your ass it has. Word on the street is that you're engaged to some stranger."

"Word on the street?"

"Okay. Okay. So your mother told me. Considering the source, you know that there was more said."

"I'm sure."

If I knew my mom, I knew that she had stretched the truth a lot.

"I'm engaged."

"To who? It's that hunk from New Orleans isn't it?"

"Yeah, and he's here."

"Already?"

"He got a job at Palagios' as a restaurant manager."

"Well at least you've got a man who's gainfully employed. So when do I get to meet him?"

"Soon I hope. I just have to run him pass my parents first."

"In that case, I'll never get to meet him. Your parents are going to eat him alive."

"I know. Dad's been polishing his rifle for a week now."

"Well, I've got to go. I've got a date tonight."

"Who's keeping the kids?"

"They're coming with. My date has a son and he suggested that we take the kids out for pizza."

"That's cool. Well, I'll holler at you later."

"Later."

I felt like I was missing out on a lot of girl time. Not to mention that I haven't seen my godchildren in months. I can only hope that I don't become a bore and confine myself to Jeff and the house. Was I giving up my youth by marrying Jeff? I certainly hoped not. The sole purpose of getting married is to be happy and totally committed to one person for the rest of your life.

That weekend, Jeff and I attended Candy Record's annual banquet. My boss said that it was imperative that I bought my husband-to-be along. I knew that my boss, Ricky, had something up his sleeve. To my surprise, the big announcement was for me. Okay so I wasn't surprised that it was for me, but I was in awe that I was now the new CFO of Candy Records.

"Rita has been an asset to our company and without her, we wouldn't be making all this money," Ricky announced.

Everyone applauded and began to chant, "Speech, Speech, Speech..." For the first time in a long time, I can honestly say that I was speechless. By the look on my face, you would have thought that I had seen a ghost. I could not believe my ears.

"Go on up there baby. This is your moment."

Jeff guided me to the stage as I stared into the crowd in amazement. Everyone looked so happy for me as if I really deserved it. This is just what I wanted. I was fresh meat and definitely had to beware of all the haters in the company. You know, the more senior members who haven't grown to the next level since they started.

I started my speech by thanking God and my family for supporting me. You know we all get religious when something good happens. Then I went on to declare my long-term goals for Candy Records. It was special that Jeff was there to share that moment with me. This was the beginning of many great memories to come.

The next morning, Jeff awoke to the sounds of vomit hitting the bottom of the toilet. It was obvious that I was overwhelmed with excitement. I couldn't eat or drink anything but water.

"Maybe you should go to the doctor," Jeff suggested.

"Oh no, honey. I'm okay. It's just all the excitement that's been going on. You get ready for work. I'll be fine."

I was off from work and I declared this day a lazy day. I didn't leave the bed for hours with the exception of trips to the bathroom. I didn't even bother to march downstairs and retrieve my mail. Jeff got it when he came home from work.

"Hey, baby. How do you feel?"

"Terrible. I think that I have a 24 hour virus or something?"

"Oh. Baby's got a little flu bug, huh?"

"It's nothing major. I took the pink stuff for my nausea and upset stomach. I just want to lay here and rest."

"Well is there anything that I can do for you, dear?"

"No. Just shower and climb into bed with me."

"What's for dinner?"

What's for dinner? I have a temperature of 109 degrees and he wants to know what's for dinner. Get real. Did he really think that I was supposed to cook under these conditions?

"Baby. In case you didn't notice. I'm sick. So you might want to order you a pizza or something."

"Oh I'm sorry. How inconsiderate of me. I'll just order take-out."

Do that you insensitive bastard. I didn't know what was wrong with me, but this fever had me moody as hell. I certainly hoped that Jeff wasn't about to drive me crazy the next couple of days.

Two days later and there I was still in bed. I should have gone to the doctor. My boss told me to take all of the time that I needed. How does that look? I get a new promotion one day and take off the next. No matter how I felt the next morning, I was taking my butt to work.

"You think it's the flu? Or maybe food poisoning? You should have gone to the doctor by now. It could be anything."

Jeff was concerned and I couldn't blame him. I had lost five pounds and would probably continue since I couldn't hold anything down.

"You're right baby. I'll get up in a minute and go visit my physician."

"Thank you. Even if it's nothing, at least you'll have piece-of-mind."

He's the one who needed piece of mind. Jeff was going to drive me crazy if I didn't get out of the house. So I guess that it would be in my best interest to go to the doctor's office.

The office was crowded and there were sick people everywhere. Dr. Renaldi had been my physician since high school and I was very comfortable with seeing him. You may have to wait all day, but he'll definitely get to the bottom of things.

"So, Ms. Rita. We meet again. Haven't seen you in a while. What seems to be the problem?"

"Well, I've been nauseated over the past couple of days and haven't been able to keep anything down. I think it's the flu."

"Well that's your first problem. You're trying to diagnose yourself. I'm the doctor. Let me be the judge."

Dr. Renaldi checked my breast, gave me a pap smear and drew blood. I said I had the flu, not an STD. What in the hell was going on?

"That's it?" I asked.

"Yes. I'm going to run some tests for now and I'll call you when the results are in."

"All of that for the flu?"

"You said that you had the flu. Not me. I'll call you in a few days, Ms. Rita. Good day."

So that's it? A stick in my tongue, a stick in my arm, a stick up my ass and that's it? Okay, now I'm worried. If I don't even know what's wrong then what do I tell Jeff? He's going to really freak out now.

"How did it go at the doctor's office?" he asked during dinner.

"He's going to run some tests and call me later in the week."

"What kind of tests?" he insisted.

"Oh you know. The usual. Routine blood tests, I guess."

"Should we be worried?"

"No, not at all. I'm not."

I was lying straight through my teeth. I was on the verge of a nervous breakdown. What was wrong with me? How could Dr. Renaldi make me wait like this? This was torture. I was better off thinking it was the flu.

Overall, I had no choice but to return to work the next day. I opened the door to my new office, only to find stacks of faxes, memos, emails, contracts, portfolios and so on. The glory days were over. Sad to say, but I was about to miss my old position. No more traveling for me. I would probably have to work through lunch and dinner, too.

"With promotion come responsibilities. Loosen up kid. It's not so bad. You'll get used to it," Rick said as he patted me on the shoulder.

How could anyone get used to this? I closed my eyes and thought about that phat paycheck that I was going to get next week.

"You're right, Rick. It's not so bad."

Problem solved. Three hundred thousand dollars a year made my job seem more and more like a bird's course by the day. Now that Jeff was working, we were bringing in enough money to pay off all of his debts. Jeff had the worse credit in the world. He only made an eighth of my salary, but I was still willing to help. In a couple of months Jeff would be debt-free. It's not like we had big bills or anything. It was easy to do.

Later that week, I received a call from Dr. Renaldi. He assured me that I wasn't sick, but he still wanted to see me in his office. I went over the next day. I wasn't worried anymore, but curious as to what he wanted to see me about.

"Dr. Renaldi will see you now," the nurse announced.

"Rita. Welcome. Please, have a seat. Your test results came in and everything's okay. Tell me something Ms. Rita. How's your love life?"

What in the hell? Was Dr. Renaldi hitting on me? Why would he ask me something like that if everything's okay?

"It's fine doctor. I'm getting married soon. We're happily engaged and everything's going well."

"I can see that Ms. Rita. You're pregnant."

"Come again?" I asked with a blank look upon my face.

"You guys are having a baby. You tested negative for everything but that. You're pregnant."

I had no immediate response. I was blank. There was nothing for me to say. I didn't know if I was happy or sad.

"So that explains why I've been so sick. How pregnant am I?"

"Well, I don't know. That's why I called you in. We have to talk and go over some dates, amongst other things. Here's a prescription for prenatal pills to get you started."

I didn't go home until late that night. I was unsure of what Jeff's reaction would be. I was unsure of what Jeff's reaction would be. I was prepared for the worse. We weren't even married yet and I was already pregnant. What would he say? I felt as if my world was about to come rumbling down.

The door flew open as I put my key in. Jeff rushed me with a big hug. His shirt was drenched in cold sweat.

"Jeff, baby, what's wrong?"

"I got off early and came home to surprise you. I know you had to see the doctor today, but that was earlier. Where have you been all day?"

"We have to talk." I began. "Come in and sit down."

My mouth was dry and I had a big lump in my throat. I was so afraid to tell Jeff what was going on. I swallowed hard and took a deep breath.

"I don't know how to tell you this, but…"

"Tell me Rita. What's wrong?"

"You're about to be a father. I'm pregnant."

"Pregnant?" He said in a whisper.

I didn't know how to take Jeff's response. He just sat there staring in thin air.

"This is good right?"

"I don't know. Is it? You don't seem too happy."

"Oh yes, Rita. I'm very happy. Just taken by surprise that's all. How are you? Do you feel okay?"

"I'm fine. That's why it took me so long to get home. I walked. Needed a little fresh air. You know?"

"Yeah baby. I know," Jeff responded as he kissed my forehead.

"So when do you call your parents?"

"I guess now. I hadn't even thought about what I would say to them."

"Look Rita. We're both making good money. Very good money in your case. We're engaged and financially stable. We're ready for a family.

So what if you got pregnant first. We'll just move the wedding up. That way we'll be married before the baby gets here."

Sounded good but it all didn't make me feel any better. Telling my parents was about to be a doozy. No point in waiting now.

"Hello?"

"Hey mom."

"Hey Rita what's up?"

"Were you sleeping?"

"Just dozed a little."

"I've got something to tell you."

"What baby?"

"I'm pregnant. Jeff and I are having a baby."

There was a long silence. For a second, I thought that she had passed out. Then I heard a sniffle.

"Oh Rita." she said in a soft tone.

"Momma don't cry. It's not so bad. I'm making really good money now and Jeff and I are about to get married."

"About! You're not married yet."

Oh boy. I knew it. Momma and her old fashioned ways. People phones were about to ring as if the circus was in town.

"So why are you crying momma?"

"I just expected more from you Rita. You can ruin your life by getting married and having a baby so young."

"You and daddy were teenagers when you guys got married. Plus you had me, and we all turned out alright."

"Back then, the best thing a Black person could do was getting married, have kids, buy a house and keep a job; Mediocre jobs at that. You have so many more opportunities. A husband and a baby can close many of those doors."

"Yeah but my three hundred thousand dollar salary can open them back up." I said with a laugh. Only momma wasn't laughing with me.

"Money doesn't guarantee happiness, Rita."

"I know momma. That's why I'm getting married. Jeff makes me happy."

"What about your job Rita? You just got that promotion."

"I'll work until the very end. I have lots of vacation and sick leave. I'll just take that when the baby comes."

"And who's supposed to keep this baby after you return to work?"

"I don't know mom. Jeff and I have a lot of talking and planning to do."

We had a whole lot of planning to do. Who knew how much confusion a baby could bring. Jeff and I battled for the next couple of weeks. From wedding dates to baby names. We finally decided to get married on Christmas. I wasn't thrilled about a winter wedding, but we had some creative ideas. Plus, we wanted the wedding to be one year and the baby's birthday the next.

My condominium was not family friendly, and we decided that we were going to buy a house. There was so much excitement in the air. The next few months were going to be a riot. Jeff and I only had a few months to go, so we had to get the ball rolling.

By the end of October, I was overwhelmed with arrangements, due dates, fees, and so on. It was obvious that I had too much on my plate. I'd have to say that out of everything, work still consumed most of my time. The baby wasn't due until next year May, and I was already considering going on maternity leave.

Jeff's main concern was my health. He didn't want me stressed. I must admit that I was surprised to see Jeff so supportive. Most men stay away when there's a baby on board.

"Rita, you just worry about the wedding and the baby. That's women stuff. I'll look for us a new house," Jeff announced.

"Well you know what our price range is, and what we're looking for. So just handle your business baby."

With Jeff being just as busy, we hardly had any time alone. My mom and Shawntee were at our place daily. On Sundays, I was smothered with a host of aunts and great-aunts. Even friends of the family wanted to have a say-so in this wedding.

With all the excitement, I knew that it would only be a matter of time, before my physician bared the bad news.

"Ms. Rita. Your blood pressure is too high. You're going to have to take it easy."

"I know. I know. But, I just have so much to do in so little time."

"I'll give you something to regulate your pressure. Just promise me that you'll take better care of yourself."

"I'll try Dr. Renaldi."

Taking it easy would require leaving all wedding arrangements up to my mom and Jeff. Now that I couldn't do. My mom would plan a country ass wedding with lace and beads and Shawntee would plan a ghetto fabulous reception buffet style. I had to figure out a way to plan a wedding, buy a house, have a baby and keep my pressure down all at once.

One of the biggest dilemmas was where to have this elaborate wedding. I personally didn't want it at the church. Our church was too small to house all three hundred of my guests.

"You can have it at my church," suggested Shawntee.

"Shawntee, you don't go to church. So what damn church are you talking about?"

"The one I got baptized in."

"When you were six?" asked my mom.

"Heifer, I'll slap you," I said with a laugh.

"Those people wouldn't know you from a can of paint."

Shawntee laughed and hunched her shoulders at my mom's gesture.

"It was just a suggestion."

"Suggests your ass downstairs and move your car out of Jeff's parking space. He should be home soon."

Shawntee returned shortly with a more clever idea. She started her announcement as she walked through the door.

"Okay, for real this time. How about at Grant Park?"

"How in the hell is she going to get married in the park? That's against the law isn't it?"

"Wait a minute mom. She might be on to something. I've heard of people doing that."

"Yeah," Shawntee continued. "You just have to obtain a permit from the City of Chicago."

"That's a good idea Shawntee. Except for one thing…the wedding is in December. We'll freeze to death dumb ass."

"At least the ceremony wouldn't last long."

My mom was growing tired and in total denial. Shawntee and I continued with the planning as she dozed in the chair. I always enjoyed watching my mom sleep. Her head hung with her chin in her chest. After a while, it would roll about forty-five degrees and her mouth would fly open. She never snored and I often would check to see if she was still breathing.

Jeff didn't get off until ten that evening. At nine thirty, I decided to send my mom and Shawntee home.

"Hey, Betty Bright Eyes. Wake up."

"I'm not sleep."

"Yes you were."

"I was just resting my eyes."

I always loved to hear my mom tell that infamous lie. Shawntee outright admitted that she was worn out. She assured me that I wouldn't see her for the next couple of days. If only my mom would have said the same.

"I'll see you tomorrow, Rita."

"See you tomorrow mom. I don't get off until six so make sure that you call first."

Jeff came home tired and whipped. I knew that sex was out of the question. The pregnancy had my hormone raging, and I was a cat in heat. I tried anyway. I hadn't gained but a few pounds and I still looked sexy in my black teddy. It had pink satin trimming with little pink bows around the thigh. The fishnet stockings and patent leather shoes set it off just right.

"Marcus, darling. I'm not wearing any panties," I said in a catcall.

Jeff and I were movie fanatics and I was sure that he knew what movie the line was from.

"Girl you are so crazy. Come here."

I pounced on him like a cheetah on her prey. For some reason, our lovemaking had become more passionate. Jeff gave me more than sex. He gave me a sense of security. When I was with Jeff, it felt as if the whole world stopped just for me. I felt no pain, knew no sorrow, and had no fears. He was my everything. He was my Prince Charming.

My new position at work was not as complex as I thought it would be. Sure my ass was flattening from sitting down all day, but I couldn't complain. My life was changing quickly, and minor alterations became apparent. Suddenly there were no more lunch breaks with Shawntee. I packed a lunch and ate alone in my office. That was the only time that I was able to isolate myself from the world.

On days where my duties were light, I would catch a two-hour nap on the chaise in my office. Aside from the wedding fiscal, others would rate my life as one big picnic. Reality is, sooner or later, the picnic would be over and I'd reap a heartburn that an over-the-counter antacid can't fix.

Fall had arrived and the colorful leaves smothered the streets. My stomach had taken shape and I was actually starting to look like a pregnant woman. It was an amazing feeling to know that a being was nestled inside of me. Jeff framed the ultrasound pictures and hung them in his office. We agreed that professional pictures of my pregnant belly would be a perfect memoir.

"We can take pictures once your stomach gets big. That'll be a nice picture to have. Don't you think?"

"I guess. It is different. What the hell. You only live once."

I went along with it. It was actually one of the best ideas that Jeff had had so far. It's just too bad that he had to turn around and ruin it.

"It can go on the front of our wedding invitations."

"I beg your pardon?"

"One of our pictures can go on our wedding invitations. I think that a black and white shot would be nice."

"You must be out of your rabbit ass mind. Then people will think that we're just getting married because I'm pregnant."

"No they won't. We had already announced our engagement before you got pregnant."

"Not formally. I am not putting my fat belly on our wedding invitations."

"Rita, a baby. The invitations go out in three weeks. You won't be that much bigger than you are now."

"Rita, you have a call on line one," the intercom interrupted.

"We'll talk about this later sweetie. I have to get back to work. I love you."

"Love you too. Bye."

Later I fed my mom Jeff's idea. Would you believe that she was actually in agreement with this fool? Two months to go. After this wedding, I'm writing everybody off. The only person that was okay in my book was my father.

"Don't listen to your crazy ass momma, Rita. You do what makes you happy. Besides, I don't want to see your fat ass stomach anyway."

"Thanks a lot daddy. That meant a lot in a loving, dysfunctional sort of way."

"You're welcomed kitten."

Later in the week, Jeff and I viewed a few houses. They were okay, but none really caught my eye. I'm not sure if it was because I didn't really know what I was looking for, or because deep down inside, I was afraid to step into the real world.

Candy Records had spoiled me, and I hated to give up my free lodging. Living in that apartment hadn't taught me real responsibility. I was so dependent on my parents and on the record company. I was starting to second-guess myself. Was I truly ready to be a wife and mother?

So, three weeks went by and the wedding invitations went in the mail. Yes. My fat belly was on it. The pictures actually came out kind of cute. I couldn't believe how nice they turned out. Twelve pounds heavier and still cute as a button. Eight pounds heavier and Jeff was too. I noticed that Jeff was gaining weight with me.

I caught him struggling to squeeze in his blazer the other day. His suits were getting kind of tight. I tried to tell him that he couldn't eat against a pregnant woman. I ate two slices of the chocolate cake that my mom gave me, and Jeff ate the other ten slices.

"I'm retaining water," he would say.

"No, man. Your ass is fat. Get it together tubby."

I ordered a size 18 dress and was starting to worry if it would fit or not. You can always take in a bigger dress, but you can't add material to a small one. The wedding was approaching and I looked as if I was pregnant with Baby Huey. Something had to give; and it did.

December flew around the corner and there I was all draped in white. Sure I'm no virgin but I was not wearing ivory for the sake of some old fashioned belief. I heard the whispers as I marched my big self down the aisle. Most of them came from the elders of the church. People kill me acting as if they've never been in the same situation. I bet you half of those old geezers were pregnant before they were even engaged. Hell, back then, women was purposely getting pregnant to trap them a husband.

Fortunately I didn't have to. I could tell by the smile on his face that I was what he wanted. I felt myself tearing as I approached the wedding party draped in black and turquoise. I was pleased with how lovely the colors turned out. Our wedding planner had schooled us on winter colors for weddings. This was better than the old-fashioned burgundy and gold or royal blue that I had seen many of times.

The reception followed the wedding and we all proceeded to the country club. Because of my membership through the company, I saved a bundle on the reception. They even included the cake, which turned out to be dazzling. Everything was so perfect. The setting was ornate and everyone truly enjoyed themselves. By the end, Jeff and I were pooped. Instead of a honeymoon, we had put all of our savings into our new home.

Jeff attempted to carry me over the threshold and we both came tumbling down. My laughter was cut short as I gasped in astonishment. The house was fully furnished. I didn't understand at first; but when I looked into Jeff's eyes, I knew that it was a gift for me.

"When?"

"Don't ask any questions, Rita. It's all for you."

"Who? I know not you."

"Oh hell no. I hired an interior decorator, girl. You know that I have bad taste."

"Well you have good taste in decorators because they did an outstanding job. I love it!"

One would assume that our evening consisted of passionate lovemaking. Not! We spent the rest of the night opening our wedding presents and cards. What do you do with three toaster, two blenders and about eight sets of champagne glasses. Cheap ones at that. One person even bought us a damn diaper bag for a wedding gift. I'm going to kill Shawntee's cheap ass.

Even through all of the excitement, there was sorrow. A somber tone hit the room and I knew that Jeff was thinking about his parents. I have never met his folks and probably never will. As long as Jeff has been in Chicago, they haven't called once. He says that he called his mother but she was upset that he had left town and moved in with a stranger. I wouldn't have been a stranger if they weren't bitter. It was obvious that they didn't want me around. It was better off not having them around anyway. I could do without the third party critics.

"Did you call them, Jeff?"

"Yeah. No one answered. I left a message and told them that we were getting married today. I even gave them the new address. Who knows, maybe they'll send a card or something."

"Here. This is a special gift for you from my daddy. He told me to give it to you once we got home."

Jeff opened the box and admired what was in it. It was my great granddaddy's pocket watch. It was of great value and very sentimental to my father.

"He would have given it to you himself but he hates mushy moments. It was his grandfather's watch. It's an antique."

"Yeah, I know. You don't find craftsmanship like this anymore. This means a lot. I'm gonna have to call him tomorrow. I think it's about time that we bonded."

"Yeah. He's your dad now, too."

"And you're my wife. Mrs. Rita Bridges. Sounds nice don't it?"

"I must admit. It compliments me well."

We gazed into each other's eyes until we dozed off to sleep. This was definitely a day to remember. The beginning of forever.

3
BABY BIRTHDAY BLUES

Now that the wedding was out of the way, it was time to plan for the little one. I had gotten pleasantly plump and the extra weight kept me warm for the winter. The house was fantastic but Jeff forgot one thing…the baby's room. We had three bedrooms and they were all decorated as guestrooms. Even our room wasn't appropriate for a child. What we needed was a nursery.

"Jeff, can't we turn one of the bedrooms into a nursery?"

"Why? Can't we just stick a crib in one of them?"

"No, I want it to look like a nursery. Stop being so cheap. Get in there and paint."

"Real cute. You know that I can't paint. Call the interior decorator. She'll hook that up."

"You just love giving your money away don't you? Are you men good for nothing these days? I tell you. When I was a little girl, my daddy did everything. He built, painted, tiled, hammered, you name it. Hell he even fried chicken in between."

"Well I ain't yo' daddy and if you want a nursery, order one. You probably can pick one right out of a catalogue."

If Jeff was nothing else, he was lazy. This was one downfall that I wasn't exposed to when we were engaged. If it were up to Jeff, he would pick up the phone and order everything from dinner to laundry. I didn't need a decorator. I could do this myself. All I needed was a gallon of paint and my best friend, Shawntee.

"Hey girl what's up?"

"Shit!"

"Ugh. You sound raunchy as hell. What's wrong with you?"

"Men! Men and flies I do despise. The more I date men…"

"The more you like flies. I feel you girl."

"What's up?"

"Well I was calling to see if you felt like getting out of the house today. I want you to help me design a nursery."

"Can't you just stick a crib in the room and call it a day?"

"You know, I'm starting to wonder if you and Jeff are related."

"I can go but I'm bringing your godchildren with me."

"That's cool. We won't be tight for long. I'm trading my car next month for a minivan."

"I didn't know that you could trade a company car."

"That's just one of the benefits of being CFO."

Shawntee and I continued our conversation on the way to the outlet mall. It was a long ride to Gurnee, but the prices were worth it. I wasn't exactly going to purchase; I just wanted to get away from Jeff for a while.

"So what's wrong, Rita?"

"Nothing. Why do you ask?"

"I know you. If you actually wanted to buy something, you wouldn't have come so far away from home. What's bothering you so bad that you had to flee."

"Okay. It's Jeff. Don't get me wrong, I love him and everything, but he's starting to smother me. I just need a little time to myself. Every time I turn around, he wants to cuddle or watch a movie. I don't want to lie in the bed all of the time. Yeah, I'm dead tired when I get off from work, but I still want to get out. The baby's not even here yet and he's trying to turn me into Aunt Jemima."

"Damn girl. I've heard of postpartum, but this is more like prepartum."

"No, it's not just the hormones talking. This man is really nuts. I can't even get up and go pee at night. He grabs the tail of my gown and asks, 'Where you going?'"

"Damn. A girl can't even take a piss? I've heard of this before. Jeff's what you call a Ritaholic."

We both burst out in laughter. When we were in high school, the boys were nuts about me. A few of them followed me around or waited for me at my locker. We called them Ritaholics. Shawntee and I always had silly labels for folks.

"Hey," I continued. "You remember Shawnteeheads."

"Yeah. I just hate that mine actually did look like crack heads."

We snickered a while and I felt a load being lifted off my shoulders. It felt good just to be me. I haven't felt this good since the wedding and that was months ago. I only had three more months to go before the baby got here and I already felt like a worn mother.

While we were out, we stopped to have dinner. The day had gone by and I'm sure Jeff had begun to worry. When I got in the car, my cell phone had eight missed calls on it. Most of them were the home number and Jeff's cell. Two of them were blocked numbers.

"I wonder who called me block."

"You don't have to wonder. Jeff called you blocked."

"You think?"

"I know."

Shanwtee was right. Jeff had left three messages and they all sounded a bit disturbing. I tried to call him back but he wouldn't answer.

"Man he must be real mad at me."

"Yeah, he's pissed. And going to eat would only add fuel to the fire. We should go straight home."

"I would if it was left up to me but it's not. The baby is hungry."

I drove to a nearby restaurant where we all enjoyed a nice sausage and cheese pizza. The kids were amazed to see me wolf down a large pizza all by myself. My appetite had picked up and I had a fat face and swollen ankles to prove it.

"Now we can go. The baby's full now."

"Girl, that don't make no damn sense. I've had kids and I never ate that much before."

"Well each pregnancy is different and my baby's a big eater."

Truth be told, I was a little larger than average. I looked above and beyond nine months. Jeff had even commented on my eating habits. It wasn't how much I ate, it was what I ate. Pizza and fries had become my best friend. So what. I wasn't big before my pregnancy and was sure to lose it fast once the baby was born.

When I got home, Jeff was furious. I had never seen him react in such a way. The rage in his eyes frightened me. It was almost as if he was a stranger.

"Where in the hell have you been all day?"

"I told you that Shawntee and I were going to the mall."

"The mall is ten miles away. Where in the hell did you go to the mall, Canada?"

"We went to Gurnee."

"Yeah, right. I guess you couldn't get a signal in Gurnee. Is that why you didn't answer the phone?"

"I left it in the car."

"Whatever."

Jeff stormed into the bathroom and I could hear his voice echo down the hall. He went on for about an hour. I couldn't believe some of the words that were coming out of his mouth.

"You must think I'm a fuckin' fool. You got me fucked up."

After he took a shower, he left the house for a while. He came in drunk with liquor. I didn't ask him where he had been. It was obvious that he had paid a visit to the local tavern. He came in apologizing and telling me how much he loved me. I charged it to the game and wrote it off as stress.

Jeff was a new husband and soon to be father. I could understand what he was going through. I was getting a little taste of it myself. Adjusting to a new city and a new way of life was hard for him. Making a marriage work was even harder. Who knew that the problems would start immediately after the wedding? I thought I got a six-month grace period or something. Damn. Somebody let a sister know what's up.

My co-workers were excited about the new arrival. They gave me a baby shower at the office. That day, I realized that I wasn't the only one making paper up in there. These people went all out. The decorations were pastel colors and the cake was in the shape of a bassinette. It was obvious that everyone had collaborated on this, because unlike my wedding, I didn't get two of the same gifts.

When I got home, I had to call in the house and tell Jeff to get all of the presents out of the car. I had everything that I needed. I don't know what my friends and family were going to be able to buy. Jeff unloaded a stroller, car seat, and diapers, even a case of baby formula. We could definitely use that. I was in the grocery store the other day and the price of formula was almost four dollars a can.

"You didn't tell me that you were having a shower at work today. You should have told me. How do you know that I didn't want to come?"

"I didn't know. It was a surprise."

"I guess they all figured you made that baby by yourself."

I didn't know where Jeff was coming from and definitely didn't want to know where he was going. I flipped the topic by asking if anyone called.

"Yeah. Some guy named Mike. Says you two went to school together."

"Oh yeah, I was wondering when he was going to call me."

"So how did he get this number? This is a new number"

"He probably called my mom and she gave it to him."

"So your momma just goes around giving out our number. Does she write it on the bathroom stalls too?"

"What is your problem? Stop tripping."

"Oh I'm tripping? Watch me trip the hell up out of here."

Okay. I don't know what's going on but either I married a stranger or it's just that time of the month. Either way it went, I was getting pretty disturbed by Jeff's performance. We were going to have a sit down once he got back home.

Three o'clock in the morning and he wasn't home. Now I was worried. Anything could have happened to him. I picked up the phone book and started calling all of the hospitals and jails looking for him. No sign of him anywhere.

He finally strolled in at sunrise. I slapped his drunken face as he entered the bedroom. There was nothing else to be said. That was it. No words spoken. I think my reaction spoke for itself.

I was so tired that I had to take a personal day from work. I felt bad to have received such nice gifts from my co-workers and employees, and then bail out on them the next day. Jeff was hung-over but he went in to work anyway. He was too ashamed to look in my face all day.

My dad came by to see me. I was surprised to see him out of the house. My dad was a hermit. He hardly came out for fresh air. He said that he had called the office and they told him that I was sick.

"Is everything alright, kitten?"

"Everything's okay daddy. Come in and sit down."

He handed be a medium package wrapped in foil. It was another cake from my mother. She knew that sour cream pound cake was my weakness. She's one of the reason's I was well over the average weight for a pregnant woman.

"You don't look sick. You look tired."

"Work's kicking my butt."

"No. That man's kicking your butt. And if he's not, he will be. You just make sure he knows that I keep the ol' pistol hot for him."

"Jeff has never put his hands on me daddy. And he won't. He's a good man. I thought you liked him."

"I accepted him. That don't mean I like him. It's something about his eyes. He never looks at me when he talks to me. His handshake is weak and he has wandering eyes. That says a lot about a man. Trust me. I know."

I was shocked to hear my dad admit that he wasn't too fond of Jeff. Maybe he just felt like nobody was good enough for his kitten. My mom admitted from day one that she didn't like him. She said that he was a liar and a cheater. Her judgment came from the way he introduced himself to her. She felt that he was arrogant and supercilious.

With all that being said, Jeff was my husband and I loved him despite how everyone else felt about him. Even Shawntee was a little skeptical. She says that he reminds him of one of her ex-boyfriends. It amazes me how everyone spoke their true feelings after Jeff and I got married. Or maybe it's just that I wasn't listening before. We sometimes filter out others' opinions to find the seed that roots our own naïveté's.

On a cool, crisp night in April, I found myself restless. For some odd reason, I couldn't sleep. I sat up all night watching television. Jeff on the other hand didn't budge. He didn't even notice that I had left the house. I took a short walk to the corner and back. I felt the need for a little exercise and fresh air. I went in to take what seemed like the longest piss ever. After a while, I decided to look in the toilet to see what was going on down there.

The toilet was filled with green urine and it was then that I realized that my water had broken. I yelled down the hall for Jeff, but he didn't answer. I wasn't in pain, but the anticipation of pain had me panicky. I wobbled down the hall and had to throw the remote control to get Jeff's attention.

"What the hell?" he said as he arose.

"The baby's on the way."

"Girl, stop playing and go back to sleep. I have to go to work in a few hours."

"I'm not playing. My water broke. We have to hurry up because it's green."

Jeff jumped up in frenzy. He tried to put his pants on so fast that he slipped and hit his eye on the corner of the dress.

"But the baby's not due for another three weeks. What did you do?"

"What did I do? I pushed the emergency release button between my legs. That's what I did. Call the hospital fool and tell them that we're on the way so that they can page the doctor."

Jeff called the hospital, while I briefly packed my hospital bag. This was something I should have down earlier in the month. I never expected the baby to come early. I don't know. It is possible that I may have calculated wrong.

The nurse patched up Jeff's eye while I suited up or delivery. She warned me the urine was green because the baby had had a bowel movement. Jeff and I never asked the sex of the baby and we didn't want to know until it arrived. Unfortunately the nurse ruined that.

"You can relax Mrs. Bridges. Your little girl won't be here for another few hours."

"Baby girl?" I asked.

"You mean to tell me that you didn't know the sex of the baby?"

"No, we never asked."

"Well congratulations. It's going to be a girl."

"Jeff. Did you here that. We're having a girl."

"I heard. What will we name her?"

"I don't know. I'll leave that up to you."

I figured that naming our daughter would be something special for Jeff. My daddy named me and we have a father-daughter bond like no other. This was our first-born and the beginning of a family. My own family.

It was strange that I didn't feel any pain. The nurse said that I was starting to have some light contractions around noon. I had been sitting there all day, and nothing. The people in the other rooms were having babies left and right. Everyone was coming up to the hospital to see me. By the time my mom arrived, I knew that she was coming to stay. I don't know who told her that I needed a damn coach.

"Hey ma'."

"Oh, look at my baby having a baby. How do you feel?"

"Fine, the nurse said that I've been having contractions but I don't feel anything yet."

"Oh but you will. They'll come out of nowhere, like lightning."

"My back just hurts real bad. I probably need some more pillows."

"How long has your back been hurting?"

"For about an hour."

"Those are your contractions, fool."

"I thought my stomach was supposed to hurt."

"Oh they'll work their way around. Trust me."

Jeff was just sitting in the corner like a lost cause. The nurse patched his eye rather dramatically and he only had use of one of them. He looked really stupid.

"What the hell happened to you?" my mom yelled.

"Don't ask."

"Don't tell. You look like a damn fool."

My mom sure had a way with words. She held nothing back. Words just flew out of her mouth like a Frisbee to a dog.

"Where's dad?"

"In the waiting room. He said he's seen enough asses in his day. He doesn't need to see yours."

Sometimes I wondered if I was adopted. My parents were great and I loved them dearly. But sometimes they were a wee bit embarrassing. You know what they say…you can't choose your family. So I guess I have to work with what God gave me.

Shortly after my mom's arrival, I started to feel the burn. I couldn't take the thought of being in pain, so I asked the doctor for an epidural. I was afraid to have that long needle inserted into my spine. I had scoliosis and was afraid that he might miss or something.

The doctor was behind me so I couldn't see what was going on anyway. What I did see was Jeff's eyes, excuse me, eye getting bigger. The poor man was terrified of childbirth. Hell, I was the one having the baby, not him. All he had to do was sit there and enjoy the show.

The epidural numbed me and I felt cold and rubbery from the waist down. At that point, I was more concerned about my looks. I could tell by Jeff's facial expressions that I looked like shit. My hair was sticking up on top of my head and my breath had to have been rank.

The nurse was polite enough to give me some mouthwash to rinse. My mom brushed my hair and oiled down my ashy feet. Jeff still sat quietly to the side. The television had been on all day and I was able to catch some of my favorite talk shows. Around four o'clock, I was starting to feel the pain and they were stronger and faster than ever.

"Uh, nurse. I think I need another one of those epidurals."

"You don't get another. The baby's on the way."

"But I can feel the pain. The point of the epidural was to take away the pain."

"I know Mrs. Bridges, but they don't last forever. You did request it kind of early. It's too late now. The baby's on the way. We can't give you anything else."

"So what is she supposed to do?" Jeff asked. It was like he had rose from the dead.

"Tough it out!" the nurse replied.

"Mom." I cried out.

"It's time, Rita. I have to go. This is you and Jeff's moment. I love you. We'll be in the waiting room."

Jeff took my hand as my mother exited the room. The television went off and a different set of bright lights was turned on. There was a long table that had been in the room all day. It was covered with blue sheets. The nurse uncovered the table and revealed an arrangement of what look like silverware for twenty. There were wire pliers, spoons, forks, knives, corkscrews and a plunger. Okay, okay. At least that's what it looked like to me.

I panicked and Jeff did too. He started hyperventilating and the nurse had to tend to him first. I had to help him through some breathing techniques. I needed for Jeff to regain his composure and keep it together.

Six o'clock on the dot and we welcomed our daughter, Sarah Ann Bridges. I liked the Sarah but hated the Ann. But I let him slide on that one since it was his grandmother's name. Sarah was seven pounds twelve ounces. She had big, bright eyes like her father, and dark curly hair. This was an experience like no other.

My mother returned to the room shortly after. She was excited to meet her first grandchild. My mom wasn't too fond of the name, but it just took some getting used to. My father remained in the waiting room until they were done stitching me up. I knew that he was eager to get into that room and see his granddaughter.

The next day, I was discharged form the hospital. They just don't do it like they used to. Back in the day, you stayed a good two to three days and got some rest. They didn't even take Sarah to the nursery. She stayed in my room the entire night. Because she was a night owl, I didn't get any rest. I was bombed when I got home the next day.

Now that the baby was here, Jeff wasn't as helpful as I thought he would be. The baby would cry at night, and Jeff wouldn't budge. I understand that he had to go right back to work, but he needed to understand that having a baby was a lot of work. It was hard for me to restore my energy. I lost a lot of blood during the delivery and had to continue to take my prenatal pills for energy.

I had a small case of postpartum depression. I felt that I was fat and unattractive to Jeff. He started taking on double shifts at work. On days that he didn't work, he hung in the bars with his co-workers.

"Jeff aren't you off tonight?"

"Yeah, but me and the boys are going to the bar. I should be home around two thirty, three o'clock."

"Can't you stay home tonight? I'm extremely tired and haven't had much rest since the baby and I came home."

"You sit on your butt all day. You're not tired, just lazy. I've been working double shifts and I'd like some chill time, too. You get to sit around, eat, and watch TV. and play with the baby all day. Let me do my thing right now."

Jeff chose to work double shifts on his own. We weren't hurting for money and it almost seemed like he enjoyed being there than at home.

Sometimes I wondered if there was another woman at his job that had caught his eye. I'm sure the women flocked to him because he was the new guy from out of town. That's how he got me. Women always like something new and something taken. Now that he had a family, he was a hot commodity.

Approaching my six-week checkup, I started searching for childcare. I hated to leave Sarah, but I had a career to get back to. My boss informed me that there was a day care located on the third floor of our office building. I made an appointment to check it out.

"Jeff, we have an appointment tomorrow to check out this day care. It's almost time for me to go back to work."

"You can go and just tell me about it later. If you like it, I love it."

"Don't you care about where your child will be going everyday?"

"I trust your judgment."

I was so surprised at Jeff. It was amazing to see just how fast a man could change on you. We haven't even been married a year and were already bickering like an elderly couple. This man had become simply impossible.

The childcare turned out to be up-to-par. I was very impressed with the advanced skills of the children. They took kids from six weeks to three year. There was even a kindergarten on the same floor. Convenience had saved me this time. I was so raring to go back to work. It was comforting to know that I would be able to check on Sarah throughout the course of the workday. It was even more calming to know that Sarah would be surrounded by other children and encouraged to enhance her mobile, verbal and learning skills over a course of time.

Rick and the other staff were glad to welcome me back. I was indeed glad to be back. Depending on Jeff for company was a no go and I had longed to be around others. I returned to work, till wearing my maternity clothes. I was still rather plump and the weight wasn't shedding as rapidly as I had anticipated.

Shawntee convinced me into enrolling in a gym near the office. This way, I could work out during lunch or immediately after work. I was hesitant at first. I told her that I wasn't ready and that the pounds would shed overtime.

"Mom, do I look fat?"

"Of course you do, honey. We all look fat after having a baby. You won't lose weight overnight."

"I know but, it's been three months already. Maybe I should go ahead and enroll in the gym, as Shawntee suggested."

"That's a good idea. Just make sure that you're doing it for you, and no one else. It's not about what others think about you. It's about how you feel about yourself."

My mom had a point. It was almost like she could read my mind. I wasn't really doing it for myself. I was actually quite comfortable with myself. It was Jeff that wasn't. You would think that he would be hornier than a toad by now. I was almost certain that he'd be ready to rumble in the jungle. Instead, he complained about how tired he was and how much his body ached from work.

Even when I tried to massage his back, he pushed me away and said that I wasn't doing it right. How was I to go about reconnecting with my husband? It was way too early in the relationship for problems. I didn't want to talk to friends or family about it. Of course they would have biased opinions based on their own relationship experiences. There had to be a way to put the fire back into the bedroom.

I was reading an article at work one day that said that it's best to get away sometimes. That was just what Jeff and I needed, sometime alone. Time away from work, the house and the baby. Everyone had been dying to keep Sarah. It was time for me to detach myself from the baby for a day and concentrate on my husband.

"Jeff, when are you off again?"

"Thursday, why?"

"We're leaving town Wednesday when you get off from work. We're going to the spa in Wisconsin."

"Where's the baby going to go?"

"My parents are going to keep her."

"That's cool. As long as we're back by Thursday night."

Now we're making some progress. All I had to do now was set the mood just right. When we arrived to the hotel, I set the candles and ran the bath. We bathed together and sipped chardonnay. Smooth jazz played over the radio and echoed into the bathroom. After the baths, we received personal massages right in the room. After our pampering for the night, I prepared for a night of lovemaking. Jeff enjoyed the little dance that I performed for him. We made love to the music and later rested in each other's arms.

Now that I had him relaxed and in a subtle state of mind, I was ready to discuss our relationship. I knew that this would be one of those rare moments that I had his undivided attention. If there was ever a time to save my marriage, it would be now.

"Jeff, honey, we need to talk."

"Last time you said that, you were pregnant." Jeff laughed.

"Well we definitely know that that's not it."

"What do you mean?"

"Jeff, our marriage is fading. You're never home. We don't spend anytime together and we haven't made love in a long time."

"We just did. And before that, you were healing from the baby."

"It didn't take that damn long to heal."

"Well I'm a man. I don't know how long it's supposed to take."

Jeff and I talked a while. I told him how I felt and he assured me that he would be more sensitive to my needs, as well as Sarah's. It was a moment of pure emotion. I knew that things would get better and felt that sense of security that Jeff had provided from the beginning.

The overnight stay had me so relaxed that I couldn't even drive back. Jeff took over the wheel while I got more rest. It was astonishing how drained a new baby could have you. Before, I knew it; we were pulling into the driveway.

"Go in the house and get in the bed baby. I'll go get Sarah from you parent's house."

The next morning, I was awakened by a loud outcry. Sarah had the cradle rocking side to side. There was no sign of Jeff. I looked at the clock on the stove. Ten thirty? I couldn't believe that I had slept so late, and so hard at that. I never heard Jeff and the baby come in that night. I never even felt him climb into the bed. It was sweet of him not to awake me when he left for work that morning.

After feeding Sarah, we took a ride downtown to walk the lakefront. There were lots of new moms jogging the lakefront with their babies. This was an interesting way to lose weight, spend time with the baby, and get some fresh air all at once. After talking with one of the joggers, I knew what type of stroller to purchase and what to pack for the jog. I took the baby by Palagios' for lunch.

I asked the waitress if she could go and get the restaurant manager for me. I wanted to surprise Jeff. I had only been to his job once. It became apparent that no one knew that I was his wife, when the waitress returned and said that he was on an important call.

"Could you tell him that his wife is here?"

"Oh I apologize Mrs. Bridges," the waitress began. "I didn't know."

I felt uncomfortable waiting while the staff stared and whispered amongst themselves. The waitress that I had previously spoken with watched me from across the restaurant. It was almost as I she wanted to say something. As if she had valuable information about my husband. Maybe I was just tripping. Shortly after, Jeff appeared from the back.

"Hey, baby, what are you doing here?" he asked as he retrieved Sarah from the stroller.

"We were out and decided to surprise you. What took you so long?"

"I was on the phone with a client. Big dinner party this weekend."

Jeff proceeded to show off the baby to his employees. For the moment, you would have thought that he was the perfect father. He sat and had lunch with us until he had to take another call.

"Look, baby, this is going to be a while. I'll just see you and the baby when I get home. I'll pickup dinner tonight so don't worry about cooking."

"Fine, Jeff."

"Hey, sweetheart. Don't sound like that. I'll see you in a few hours."

As time went by, I wondered if it was the baby that caused our relationship to deteriorate. He hadn't developed a relationship with Sarah. It was almost as if she was mine and mine alone. If Jeff didn't want a family, then he should have left a long time ago. I'd rather had stayed single mom with a bastard child than put up with Jeff's bullshit.

Palagios' started hosting more parties and it was all Jeff's bright ideas. This premier restaurant was turning into an elite nightclub. This was just another one of Jeff's escapes from home. At times, Jeff would come in at four, five in the morning, pissy drunk. Not only was it unprofessional but disrespectful to his family. According to Jeff, it was about business, not pleasure.

"If you don't drink and party with these associates, they find it degrading. This could cost me the accounts. I have to leave a lasting impression on these people so that they will keep coming back."

Jeff's lies became repetitive and redundant. I knew that there was more to the story, but I just couldn't prove it. I had a job of my own and just didn't have the time to invest into Jeff's drama. The best thing was to ignore him and concern myself with Rita, Sarah and Candy Records.

I started to put more energy into my work. I took an interest into the many different departments in the corporation. Everyone loved Sarah and bringing her around was a joy. She took away the sorrow that Jeff had introduced to my heart. People always say look at the better side of things. Sarah was the better side of Jeff. She was my only connection to him. It was as if our marriage had become void. Which is why I wasn't surprised when Jeff forgot our wedding anniversary.

"Most people forget after the first five years, Jeff. Not the first year."

"I know, Rita, I'm sorry. I've just been so consumed with work that it slipped my mind. We can still go out."

"Forget it, Jeff. You do whatever it is you do and I'll just stay home with the baby."

"No. I can't have that. We're going out. Call your mom and see if she'd keep the baby."

"Really, Jeff. I'm in a sour mood now and it would be ridiculous for us to even sit in public together."

"Damn. It's that bad?"

Jeff made the statement as if it almost amused him. By the way I felt, I could have hauled off and smacked that stupid ass smirk off of his face. Jeff and I had never really had words, and I wasn't going to start. Instead, I used guilt to eat at him.

"I'm going to bed. Your gift is in the kitchen on the table."

Suddenly, the situation wasn't so amusing anymore. It was evident that he was ashamed to even go into the kitchen and open the gift. I checked on the baby and proceeded to the room to take off my dress. All dolled up for nothing. My dress hit the floor and I hit the bed.

Jeff sounded like a mouse in the kitchen, unwrapping his gift. I could hear him swear as he uncovered his new laptop computer. A picture of Sarah and I served as a screensaver. The front door echoed as Jeff left the house. He never said a word to me that night. He never came home either. I cried awhile until I was fast asleep.

The next morning, there was a box lying beside the bed. Attached was a note that read,

"Sarah, nothing in this world could compare to what you have given me. I have been such a jerk and unappreciative of the unconditional love that you've provided. I know that there's nothing that I could do to make up for the way I've treated you. I just want you to know that I love you (and Sarah) and there's nothing or no one that can take that away. Please accept my apology so that we can move on, together. Love Always, Jeff."

I unwrapped the box and in it was a family ring. It had all of our birthstones on it. Tears gathered in my eyes as I tried it on. I didn't know whether to be happy or concerned. I didn't feel that Jeff's plea was sincere. I knew that it was only going to be good for a short period of time.

We made it through the winter months okay. Jeff had become more attentive to Sarah now that she was beginning to walk. He spent more time with her and often took her with him. Although he was adapting to fatherhood, he still wasn't the husband that he declared to be.

He often reminded me of the material things that he's bought me. He couldn't grasp the concept of love. Taking me shopping was his way of loving me. Diamonds and fur coats didn't ease the pain that I felt when I saw couples walking up the street or even grocery shopping together. It was the little things that made me happy.

He offered to workout with me at the local gym. I felt offended because I knew that my weight had become the latest issue. It has been a year and I was now up to two hundred pounds. Big difference from one thirty nine. Sometimes, I would catch a glimpse of Jeff staring at me as if in disgust. My husband was no longer attracted to me and I knew that I had to make some changes to save my marriage.

I signed up for some classes during my lunch break. The gym was on the eighth floor of the office building. I even cut back on my eating and took the stairs at work. I was willing to give this weight loss plan my all. I wanted Jeff to admire my body jut as he did two years ago.

Coming up to Sarah's birthday, I had started to lose. I wanted to step it up with a diet pill but my physician said that it would negatively react with my birth control. Jeff hadn't noticed yet, but people on the job had started to compliment me. My mother had even said that I was starting to shed a few pounds.

Preparing for Sarah's party was stirring for me. This was her first birthday and I was committed to making each one special. Shawntee thought that I was going to put the party store out of business.

"Damn, girl. You've bought up everything, now let's go."

"We can go drop some of these things off but I have two more stores to go to. These are just the decorations. I haven't bought her gifts yet."

"Gifts? My kids always get just one gift."

"Well most of it will be her summer wardrobe. I'm buying her a new playpen and a few toys. It's mostly stuff that she needs anyway."

"What did Jeff want to get her?"

"I don't know. He said that he had a special gift for her. Who knows? I know Jeff, I know that there's a piece of jewelry involved."

"Jewelry for a one year old?"

"You'd be surprised. Jeff's a show-off. He like for people to ooh and ahh over the things that he do. It's all for show."

I knew that Jeff had something flashy up his sleeve. I figured that he was trying to out-do me. As if it was a competition or something. Everything always had to be about Jeff. Even our daughter's birthday.

The weather was pleasant the day of the party. It wasn't too cool to be outside. I had the backyard and patio decked out. The kids had a ball. Sarah was having fun until the clown arrived. I had no idea that he would be frightening to a little child. Sarah wasn't having it. She climbed into her grandmother's lap and watch from a distance. While the clown entertained the children, I went inside to call Jeff.

"Jeff where are you. It's almost time to open the presents."

"I'm sorry baby. I had to stay a little late today. I'll be there shortly."

It amazed me how Jeff chose work over his child's birthday. It was apparent that Jeff was lying. I overheard a woman's voice in the background as he hung up the phone. We all sang happy birthday and ate cake. Jeff arrived right at the end of the opening of the gifts.

"Sorry I'm late. Happy birthday Sarah."

He opened a little box and place a pair of diamond studs into Sarah's ears. Unsurprisingly, everyone ooh and ahhed over his presentation. I cut my eyes at Shawntee to gesture an, "I told you so". Nothing Jeff did at this point surprised me. After all I had done, he would come in and steal the glory.

"That was some performance Jeff put on, huh?" my mom asked on the phone later that night.

"Yeah, some performance."

"Where is he now?"

"Had to get back to work of course."

"Of course."

I wasn't the one to put people into my business, but I felt the need to confide in my mother. I turned her about the many issues that I had been fighting with Jeff. She told me similar stories about her and dad. She assured me that it happens in all marriages and that was just how some men were. I begged to differ.

Jeff wasn't your typical man. There had to be more behind his actions. Did I think that there was another woman? Of course. But when it came to Jeff, I didn't feel that he would do his dirt so close to home. It wasn't the obvious that concerned me. It was the unknown.

4
JEALOUS RIGHT HAND MAN

Who knew that stress would be the cause of my weight loss? People were right. There is a better side to things. I was almost at my normal weight, with the exception of bigger boobs. I looked like a real life Jessica Rabbit. My male co-workers were suddenly more interested in Rita and the women were persistent in their catcalls. I was back!

With my amazing body came a newfound freedom. Jeff didn't know what had hit him. It was like out of the blue I was hot again. Even my mom and Shawntee were amazed at my sudden weight loss. I had regained my self-esteem and even developed a bit of a diva attitude. My energy was boosted and I was back running the streets.

"Where are you going?" Jeff inquired as I dressed for the nightlife.

"In case you haven't noticed, It's my birthday. Uh huh. Pick your jaw up sweetie. I'm sure that you forgot that too. Which is why I've made plans for myself."

"Well that's cool. Just let me get dressed."

"No. I have plans. They don't include you. I think that you need to stay home and think about what you're risking. Oh yeah, and you might be developing an early case of Alzheimer's."

"Who's keeping the baby?"

"Nobody. She's staying at home with her loving father. Don't wait up."

I kissed him on the top of his head and headed straight for my car. I smiled and waved as I left him standing in the front door with his baby in his arms.

It felt good to be out again. The D.J. announced that it was my birthday and rounds of drinks started flowing in. I was getting much needed attention from all of the men. Attention that I had yearned from my husband.

The girls and I were falling over by the end of the night. We were all too drunk to drive so we decided to crash at Shawntee's house. She was the only one who didn't have a husband. Everyone else's home was off limits. Jeff was off the next day, so there was no rush to get home. Shawntee fixed coffee and we socialized for hours.

"Okay. I have to get home to my baby now. I'm sure she misses me."

"You miss her more than she misses you. She's probably having a ball."

"With who? Not her daddy. He probably has her in the walker, scooting around and tearing up the house."

What had I done? Was I crazy to leave Sarah at home with her father? Sure that's her dad, but will he give her the attention that I've provided for almost two years now? I pictured my baby lying in the crib, screaming and crying. He probably hadn't even fed her today. I rushed home to see about my child.

When I walked in, the house was silent. No one was home. Where had Jeff gone with the baby? I called my mother and she said that she had the baby.

"Jeff bought her last night. He said that he was taking you out for your birthday."

"Mom, I went out with the girls last night. Jeff forgot it was even my birthday. I'm on the way to come and get her."

I could not believe this. I had expected what I thought was the worse. Apparently not. How could he be so deceitful? I swooped by my parents place and grabbed the baby. On the ride there, I tried to contact Jeff several times, but there was no answer. I even called the restaurant to see if he had to come in on his day off. Nope.

The tables had turned and I ended up being the one to sit up all night and wait. The next morning, I awoke to an empty bed. I called the restaurant again and they said that he had called off. That son-of-a-bitch had time to call off but no time to call home? I wanted to search for him, catch him in the act, but I didn't know where to begin.

His employees weren't helpful and my family hadn't a clue. Two days went by and Jeff finally stumbled his way into the house. He reaped of alcohol and cheap perfume. He had on clothes that I had never seen before.

"Where in the hell have you been?"

"Out."

"Out where? Did you forget that you had a family to come home to? Did you forget that you had priorities?"

"Did you forget? You wasn't thinking about priorities when you stayed out all night. You probably was laid up with another man."

"I went out with the girls. You know that. What sleazy tramp did you sleep with last night?"

"Don't ask me shit. I was with whomever you were with on your birthday. Don't ask me any fucking questions."

Jeff pushed me on the sofa as he stumbled past. He was so drunk that he had pissed on himself. He finally made it to the bed and passed out.

I was fiery red. There was only so much that I could take, and this was it. I went in the kitchen and filled a pitcher with cold water. While he was sleeping, I examined his body. There were purple hickies that led from his neck to his private parts. I picked up his cell phone and scrolled through his outgoing and incoming calls. There was one last number left from my birthday. I went into the bathroom and called the number from his phone.

"Hey baby," a voice answered. "Home already?"

"Who's this?" I asked.

"Who is this?"

"This is Jeff's wife."

There was silence and then a click. The woman on the other end had hung up. I attempted to call her back several times, but she wouldn't answer. I wrote down the number and put it up for later. As I entered the bedroom, I grabbed the pitcher of cold water and poured it all over Jeff's face.

"Get your pissy ass out of my bed and take a shower."

"What in the hell is your problem?"

"I called your bitch. The bitch hung up in my face. Who is she?"

"I don't know what the hell you're talking about."

"Oh yeah. What's with all of the hickies on your body? How'd you get those?"

"Who told you to go through my phone? I don't have time for this shit. I'm getting the fuck up out of here."

He grabbed his keys and stormed out the front door. I knew that he was headed straight to her house. I put the baby in the car and followed him. He saw me in the rear view mirror and decided to detour back to the house. We slept in different rooms that night. Now I see why we needed a house with three bedrooms.

I took all of my frustrations out at the mall. I started purchasing more expensive clothes, and even decided to buy new furniture for the house. True enough, I was spending unnecessary money but it was either that or start eating again. Sarah and I spent more time at the office building and away from home. Going home everyday was more depressing than ever.

Jeff's drinking had become uncontrollable. He would come home and want to fight for no reason at all. I could tell that the other woman was beginning to piss him off. I wanted to confront her, but that would only heighten the drama.

"Do you know who she is?" asked Shawntee.

"Priscilla Wooddale. 1515 E. Glendale Rd. Apt. 1A."

"How long have you known this, Rita?"

"Quite some time now. I've been by there on several occasions and saw his car parked in the lot. I just never confronted her."

"Girl, if that was me, I would have rung the doorbell and whipped her ass in her own house."

Why is it that when you're having issues your girlfriends always want to tell you what they would do in that situation? And know that they're lying, too. If she were in my shoes, she'd do the same thing that I was doing. Contemplating!

"I don't know anything about this woman. I'm sure that he probably didn't tell her that he was married. If he lied to me, he probably lied to her too."

"Well if she didn't know, why did she hang up in your face?"

Shanwtee had a point. It was almost as if the woman knew me or knew of me. I was determined to at least see what she looked like. I bet she was cute and young. She probably didn't have children and still had her high school figure. Or maybe she was an older woman: Someone a little closer to his age. Whoever she was, I had to see her.

I convinced Shawntee to go with me. I couldn't drive my car because Jeff would recognize it if he was there. We snoozed around a couple of times before we finally saw her. Jeff arrived at the apartment complex during the hours that he was supposed to be at the restaurant. To my surprise, I recognized the young lady that was exiting on the passenger side. There she stood, the young waitress from the restaurant. She opened the back door and a little girl got out. Jeff was playing house with another woman.

"Damn. What you gone do girl?"
"I don't know. Should I get out? And if I do, what would I say?"
"You don't say shit. You just start whipping ass."
"There's got to be another way Shawntee."
"Cut the 'I'm a lover not a fighter' bullshit and whip that bitch ass."

I was stuck between a rock and a hard place. I didn't know what to do. I was baffled at the thought of my husband spending quality time with what seemed to be his other family. Men are scandalous. Living a double life right under my nose. Seeing this sure explained a lot.

Confronting him right then and there was out of the question. I had to rethink some things. I refused to let one incident change my outlook on marriage. There just had to be a better way.

"So what you gone do heifer?" Shawntee insisted.
"I'm going home."
"Going home?"
"Yeah. I'll deal with Jeff when he brings his ass home."

Dealing with him was an over-statement. I wasn't prepared to do anything. Needless to say, I wasn't prepared for another woman. Deep down inside, I prayed that this would all go away. But it didn't. My distrust and insecurities grew stronger by the day. I never made Jeff aware of my knowledge of his affair. Instead, I just balled up and cried while he volunteered lie after lie. There was nothing I could do. After all, he was my husband and the father of my child. We were a family.

I had to accept it and put it in the back of my mind in order to make it work.

Bullshit! What kind of fool did he think I was? I allowed Jeff to go on for a while, hoping that he would come clean about his infidelities. But he didn't. Why would he? I'm sure that in his mind it was a, don't ask don't tell situation.

Jeff got dressed one evening for a business dinner, so he called it. On his way out he said,

"I'll be out late Hun. Don't wait up."

"Sure baby. Oh yeah, tell Priscilla I said hello, and hope she's enjoying the ride."

Jeff stopped dead in his tracks. He was at a lost for words. He turned slowly only to reveal the truth on his face.

"What ride?"

"Don't play me. That whore is riding you like a roller coaster at the fair. Every night! Every night that you proclaim to have worked late."

"You're tripping. I'm not even interested in that little ass girl."

"You seemed pretty interested in her little girl."

"What in the hell? Have you been following me?"

"Don't worry about that. But if I come up to that restaurant tonight and there's no meeting, that's your ass and that ashy ass bitch's."

Jeff contemplated for a quick second, looked at his watch, then removed his blazer.

"I'll be on the porch."

"Yeah. Go call the bitch and tell her you can't come out tonight."

He sat on the porch and smoked a cigarette. About an hour later, I heard him in the kitchen pouring a drink. I must have startled him when he turned around and found me standing in the doorway.

"So this shit got you all fucked up huh?"

"Not really. She didn't mean anything to me. Things just haven't been the same since you got pregnant. I was ready for marriage but not a baby. I guess I should have told you that before you got pregnant."

"You think? Or maybe you should have taken the proper precautions to prevent us from having this baby?"

"Well, for what it's worth, I'm sorry."

"Don't be sorry too many times."

I turned around and headed towards the room. Jeff grabbed the bottom of my gown and reeled me in. This was the perfect moment for make-up sex. Not for me. I couldn't block images of Jeff making love to the waitress. I felt strange making love to my own husband. Almost violated. I felt as if I had been raped of my most prized possession, my husband.

I stopped ten minutes into four play and asked Jeff to get off of me. He had the most confused look on his face.

"What's wrong?"

"I can't do this. The thought of you with another woman devours me right now. It's all that I can think about."

"I understand. It's going to take time."

"That and an HIV test."

"What?" he asked abruptly.

"I don't know if this bitch is clean or not. As a matter of fact, I'm coming to the restaurant to talk to her and I'm bringing a pregnancy test with me. I would ask you to fire her, but that's opening the door for a sexual harassment case."

"Don't come to my job. I'll talk to her and put an end to all of this."

"Like hell you will. And in case you try to send her home, or warn her to call off, I have her address. Now try me if you want to."

I turned off the lamp and we laid there in silence. I could feel Jeff's breath on my face while he stared at me in fury. I didn't care. He feared me because he had never seen me so angry. At this point, he didn't know what to expect from me.

The next day had to be hell for Jeff and Priscilla. I'm sure that he gave her the run down first thing in the morning. Unfortunately, I didn't show. It was more enjoyable just knowing that they both were on guard all day long. This marked a pattern for a few weeks. Jeff all of a sudden became more in tuned to my needs. If he communicated with Priscilla at all, it was during business hours only.

Jeff kept a clean record for about three months. He had me going for a minute. Just when I had congratulated him on his efforts, things had to go wrong. I received an unexpected phone call one evening while Jeff was out.

"Hello?" I answered.

"It's ten o'clock, bitch! Do you know where your husband is?"

"Who is this?"

"Jeff's woman. You know who I am."

"So what is it that you want with me?"

"Just thought that you should know that Jeff loves me, not you. He's in my shower right now. You might as well leave now before you get your feelings hurt. Pretty soon, your house and husband will be mine."

I cleared my throat as I sat up straight in the bed. There was a short silence so that I could assure that I had her undivided attention.

"That is your opinion and you're entitled to it. It is neither required nor desired. So think again, bitch."

"Oh, we'll see real soon."

"Your eyes may shine, your teeth may grit, but this nice house, you will not get. Just a little nursery rhyme for you, kid. Get a life."

I had been tested and pushed to the limit. If Jeff couldn't control his bitches, then I would. It's one thing to do dirt, but it's another when your dirt follows you home. I knew that it was time for me to reveal myself to both Jeff and Priscilla.

No matter how hard you try to be professional, someone's always got to bring the hood out of you. I didn't want to have to cut anyone, so I had to become more creative in my thinking. Shawntee suggested that we get her fired. This was a bad idea considering Jeff could lose his job as well. I had something cleverer up my sleeve. It was only a matter of time before the situation would be confronted.

"Hello, Priscilla. This is Rita, Jeff's wife. I don't want any trouble. I just want to talk. You know, woman to woman."

She was young and it was a sure bet that she would fall for the okee-doke. We met one evening while Jeff was at the gym working out. I was dumbfounded when I discovered that she was only nineteen and Jeff was helping her pay bills.

"Jeff said that you two were about to get divorced and he was going to marry me. I didn't even know that he had a baby until you two came into the restaurant that day."

"Yes, well, Jeff is very married, but there's no divorce. At least not yet. You couldn't possibly think that this man would leave his family, house, cars, everything, for you could you?"

"That's what he told me. And I believe him. He said that you had gotten fat after the baby and he lost attraction to you. He also said that you thought that you were better than everyone else."

Why is it that women always believe what the man says? A married one at that. No fool in his right mind would give up everything for a piece of ass. I gave her the benefit of the doubt because she was young and had a child. It was clear that no one her age wanted to be bothered with her and she was merely looking for a baby-daddy.

"I'll tell you what, Priscilla. I understand that you're young and you feel that you need a man in your life right now. I'll grant you the presence of my husband for as long as he allows. But I promise you, that won't be very long. So get all the bubble gum money you can get. Pretty soon, the well will run dry, cause all that money's coming home to mamma."

She went into frenzy and decided to curse me from head-to-toe. It was all right though. I didn't have to deal with her anymore. She told me everything that I needed to know. She had become panicky and nervous. Her ends were about to come up short and she knew that she would have to squeeze Jeff dry before I did. This would only piss him off and drive him away.

See, it's alright when a man only have to nickel and dime it; nickel for your nails, a dime for your hair. No man just outright volunteers to pay your bills and take care of your baby. So don't think for one second that he loves you because he got your hair done, nails done, and paid your cell phone bill.

I had to fight fire with fire. Jeff had noticed my revealing business wear and started to ask questions. I was giving the men at work a little eye candy and they loved it. Jeff hated it. He accused me of sleeping with my, which even he knew that it was a bit far-fetched. I worked very hard to get that position and I wasn't going to allow Jeff to question my talent.

"Where are you going?" Jeff asked as I dressed for the evening.
"We're going out. Get dressed."
"What about the baby?"
"Shawntee's keeping her."
"We have to take her all the way to Shawntee's house?"
"No she's coming here. We're staying out for the night."

"Where are we going?"

"Stop asking so many questions and just get ready."

We drove about an hour to Joliet. Going to a nearby suburb is like leaving town for married people with children. At dinner, Jeff was on me like glue. I was looking good and had an audience to prove it. Men pranced past our table several times, complimenting Jeff on what a beautiful wife he had. I was surprised at how bold men have become. Jeff was like my bodyguard that night. It took a handful of complimentsfor him to realize what he really had.

"You are really wearing that dress tonight. I'm not just saying that because ten men have said it already. You really look good."

"Thank you, baby. You don't look so bad yourself. Remember what we wore on our first date."

"Which one? The one where I didn't show, or the one where you blew me off?"

"The one where we both were civilized."

We laughed and reminisced the night away. The more we talked about our past sexual experiences, the more we realized what was missing. We both had become boring in the bedroom. We had become routine in our sexual practices. You'll be surprised how easy it is to lose the spice, after being with someone for a while.

Jeff had lost all of the seasoning in our dressing and left with nothing but cornbread. It was time we searched for a little say and cream of chicken. We stopped at a nearby sex shop on the way to the hotel. It was fun laughing and playing around with the novelties. Jeff was actually interested in purchasing some gadgets; so we did.

It was strange trying this sort of thing out for the first time. We fumbled for a while, but then we got it. I'd have to say that it was an experience like no other. This was definitely a sacred moment for husband and wife. I'd like to see the nineteen year old top that. She'd probably think that she'd get cancer from the batteries.

Our overnight stay was definitely educational and refreshing. On our way back, we returned to the shop to stock up on some more of the freaky stuff. We laughed and talked while sitting in rush hour traffic. I had Jeff right where I wanted. He was acting right, feeling right, and there was no better time to ask...

"Baby, can you buy me a mink coat?"

"Sure."

"Before Christmas. Like this month?"

"I don't know, Rita. We'll have to see what the budget looks like."

"You can afford it. I'd just love to show everyone at work what my husband bought me."

Men loved for you to flaunt their gifts. A man can buy you something once a year, and will talk about it for the next five. That one gift is Christmas, Birthday and Valentine's Day all in one. Especially considering Jeff was poor at remembering dates.

Aside all of that, the main goal was to get Jeff to spend the bulk of his money on me. Don't get me wrong; it's not about material things. The plan is to take his attention (and money) away from Priscilla. The less she gets, the more she complains. The more she complains the more pissed off Jeff gets.

Needless to say, I was being very devious. But you must admit, it was clever. I was certain that this would work. If I knew Jeff, I knew that he hated a nag. I can't say that I like playing games with this girl, but I was determined to get her out of our lives.

"Shawntee I tell ya'… If it ain't one thing it's another."

"I know, girl. I've been down this road before and I'm sure it's got to hurt a hell of a whole lot worse because you're married. What is this world coming to?"

"It's been like this since biblical days. Men just like sex. Old sex, new sex, young sex. You name it."

"Well it's not always just about sex, Rita. How do you make him feel? Do you actually treat him like a man?"

"Of course I do. What kind of a question is that? I respect my husband."

"What I'm saying, Rita is that men like to be wanted and needed. If you don't need him, then he feels he has no purpose."

"Shawntee, I make a lot of money. I was making a decent salary when I met him. The only thing that I need Jeff for is companionship. Hell, I'm barely getting that."

"Well you need to learn how to act like you need him. If you don't, you're going to drive him into the arms of another woman."

"By not needing him? What type of bullshit is that?"

"It's what's real. He feels like he's not good enough for you. If you can handle everything yourself, then what's he sticking around for? I'm telling you, this is how men think."

Shawntee had a point. Jeff has been throwing it in my face about how I make more money than him. Our bills are paid and he's doing so well on his job. I never once thought that Jeff had some insecurity in the relationship. He hadn't said anything to me about it. If he has, it was indirectly.

Jeff had been coming home on time for the next couple of weeks. There was no word from Priscilla either. I never questioned it anymore. I was afraid that the tables would turn and I'd end up being the nagging bitch. Jeff had given in to all of my requests, including the full-length mink that I asked for. So technically, what was there to complain about?

"Rita, I need to talk to you when I get home from work. It's important."

"Well why can't we talk now?"

"No, not now. Later."

I had no clue as to what was pondering Jeff. It had to be serious because his veins were popping out his forehead like fireworks on the fourth of July. While at work, I speculated what the problem may be. I hadn't a clue as to what was about to go down.

When the baby and I got home, Jeff had set the table for dinner. I was relieved to see that he had bought something home from the restaurant. I was too exhausted to cook. We ate in silence and I was hesitant to spark the conversation.

"So what did you want to talk about, honey?"

Jeff looked at Sarah sitting in her high chair and rubbed his hand over her curly hair. He gazed at her for a while before he spoke.

"Man, she growing up so fast."

"Yeah, pretty soon we'll be sending her to college."

"You remember when she was born? She looked like a pale ghost. Everything about her was different. She didn't look like you or me. Hell, she didn't look like anyone."

"This is true."

"But now she's starting to develop her own look. She has some of your features but she looks nothing like me."

"So what are you saying?"

"I'm not stupid, Rita. Sarah's not my child."

"You wait until she's almost two before you say something. You know damn well this is your daughter, how dare you?"

"Don't go there, Rita. This baby looks like some other man, but not me."

"Fine, dammit! We'll settle this with a paternity test. And when the test proves that you're the father, we're going straight to Priscilla's house."

"Here we go. So what you think Priscilla's daughter is mine now?"

"No, stupid. You haven't even been in Chicago that long. We're going to end your little rendezvous once and for all."

"This is about Sarah right now. I want to know who you were messing around with."

"Your daddy. Asshole."

I was highly upset after dinner. How dare he deny his child like that? Jeff knew the truth but he insisted that I had been with someone else. I wouldn't be surprised if he assumed I was sleeping with my boss. Jeff had some hidden animosity against my boss.

I didn't hesitate to call and schedule an appointment for a paternity test. Dr. Renaldi was alarmed by my phone call.

"Ms. Rita, are you absolutely sure that your husband's the father of this child?"

"Entirely!"

"Well have your husband come in and see me this week. Have him to bring the baby with him."

I was so pissed that I just left a note on the refrigerator with the appointment and directions to the physician's office. The day of the test I decided to sit out. Jeff took Sarah to the doctor's with him. Dr. Renaldi called to alert me that Jeff and Sarah was on their way home.

The night was glum and I retired for bed early. Jeff slept on the sofa with Sarah by his side. I could overhear Jeff singing to her. It was obvious that he was starting to regret denying his only child. Two more days and he would know for certain that Sarah was truly his daughter.

The next day was awkward. Jeff volunteered to keep the baby with him for the day. I'm ashamed to say that I was afraid that Jeff was going to harm or displace our child. I was nervous to go to work and leave my child behind. I trusted her more with the people at the day care than I did with her own father.

"I'd hate for her to play hooky from school at such a young age. Maybe she should go. We pay too much for childcare for her to be missing school."

"It's one day. I'm sure that they'll be glad to have one less child crying all day."

Jeff finally convinced me to let her go with him for the day. I called the house several times to check on them. Jeff had taken her out for chicken nuggets. They were one of the few finger foods that she enjoyed. I wondered what Jeff was thinking in the back of his head. He sure didn't seem nervous while he awaited the test results. I could only pray that things would get better after the paternity test came back. I just wanted a normal family. Everything was becoming dysfunctional between us.

Dr. Renaldi called and requested that only Jeff came into the office. I have been acquainted with my physician for a long time and was offended when he only wanted to see Jeff. This was a family crises and I needed to know the results just as he did. There was no doubt in my mind that Jeff was the father, but all of this secrecy had me second-guessing myself.

Jeff returned a new man. He had a big teddy bear for Sarah and roses for myself. He fell before me and begged my forgiveness. Sarah was his daughter all along. He seemed so relieved and at that moment, I could feel that things were going to be alright.

"I love you two so much. I'll never doubt you again, Rita. And tomorrow, we're going to Priscilla's house. I'm going to tell her that I'm never going to see her again."

I knew that that wasn't completely possible because they worked together. It was up to Jeff whether he wanted to save this family or not. I wasn't sure how hard it was going to be for him to get rid of Priscilla, and I didn't care. We were definitely addressing the issue the next day.

Sarah went to my mom's house while Jeff and I were at Priscilla's. Jeff called her phone to let her know that he was on the way. He didn't alert her that I was with him. She buzzed him and I followed behind. Her jaw dropped when she saw me walk through the front door.

"Priscilla, we meet again."

"What in the hell are you doing here?"

"Priscilla, my wife and I came to talk to you like adults, so sit down and act like one."

She offered us a seat and begins asking questions as to what was going on. Jeff gave her a speech about how he was just going through a phase and didn't really love her. Priscilla started to weep as he went on about his priorities and being there for his family. I even felt a bit of sorrow as I saw this young woman pour her heart out to him.

I knew the hurt that she felt and there was nothing that could save her from it. It was a part of like. We all have to hurt at some point in our lives, especially when transitioning into adulthood. She raved a while, and then her young daughter joined her. It was as if they had death in their family.

Jeff had become a father figure to this child and she had grown quite fond of him. I was in awe when she asked him...

"Daddy, are you ever coming back?"

Daddy? I can't believe that he had this little girl calling him daddy, and that her mother would allow it. You never introduce a man into your daughter's life if he's not going to be there for the long hall. And the only way that you know that is if he puts a ring on your finger. Hell, that doesn't guarantee anything these days.

Situations like this can ruin a little girl forever. This will affect how she view men when she gets older and start dating. This was something Priscilla needed to concern herself with. They both cried out to him and my heart cried out to them. I snuck out the front door so that they could get their last goodbyes in.

5
SUDDEN SEPARATION

Jeff and I finally got to take a real vacation. We went to the Bahamas for a few days. He had finally been on his job long enough to accumulate some vacation time. Life was getting a whole lot better for the both of us. Sarah was three now and moving on up the preschool ladder. She had developed a lot of skills in daycare and was growing more and more by the day.

Priscilla had decided that she couldn't work with Jeff anymore and went on to another restaurant. We wished her well and I gave her a little woman-to-woman advice. She was certain that she wasn't going to get involved with married men anymore. She had also learned her lesson about bringing men into her daughter's life.

The beaches were beautiful and Jeff looked tempting in his swim trunks. It took me back a couple of years to when I first met him. He was the finest thing I had ever laid eyes on and still is. I loved him so much and was glad that our lives were back on track. He was my husband and I didn't want to lose him.

"Come on in. The water's warm," he yelled from a distance.

I ran toward him and leaped in for a dive. I was a great swimmer and hadn't swum in years. We don't get beach weather back home. There was just something so relaxing about opened water. It's far better than indoor swimming pools.

We had timeshare in the Bahamas and our beach house was right on the beach. Jeff did all the cooking and pampering that week. It was like heaven on earth. I dreaded going back to Chicago at the end of the week. We did start to miss Sarah, though.

We had our film developed before leaving the Bahamas. Jeff and I viewed them as a past time during our flight. This was the first trip to be added into our family photo album.

"We should plan to take at least two trips a year," I suggested.

"That sounds good. We'll just pre-plan them so that I can put in my vacation time."

"One will just be for the two of us and the other trip will be for Sarah."

"She's so young. Would she remember any of them?"

"We'll make scrapbooks for all of the trips. She'll have pictures of the ones that she doesn't remember."

We spent hours talking about our trip. Afterwards, we talked about our future plans as a family. Jeff and I have made great process, financially, and now it was time to do something with it.

"I was thinking about investing in stock. You know, together."

"What, you already have stock?" he asked.

"I have some money invested into Candy Records."

"So you work like a dog for them and then give the money back?"

"No. I make a great salary for the work that I do. It's not like I'm volunteering my services. And yes I have shares in the company's stock. It's a part of our employee benefit plan. You should check into the restaurant and see what extra incentives they have."

"No need. I was thinking about buying a building and renting the apartments."

"That's a good idea. Two or three flat?"

"I was thinking about a court way."

"The only thing about court ways is that they require much more maintenance and it costs more for repairs. Plus, a lot of Chicago's court ways are very old and have those old, really expensive furnaces and water tanks. If one breaks down, it's going to cost a fortune to have a newer model installed."

"Why is it that when I have an idea, you always have to tear it down?"

"I'm not tearing it down. I just think that that's something that you need to look into before making a decision."

"So what, I'm stupid now? You think that I can't make wise decisions when it comes to an investment?"

"Look, Jeff. We're just coming in from a wonderful vacation. Let's not start."

"Oh so now it's me starting?"

"Jeff. Please?"

We retrieved our bags from the baggage claim and caught a cab home. The cab was expensive but it was much cheaper than it would have cost us to leave our car at the airport all week. The weather was nice and the trees were bending. I was glad to leave, but happy to be back. Sometimes we all have to escape our normal lives and break free.

Sarah was glad to have her parents back. I was certain that my parents had kissed her to death and had given her a sugar overload. When we dropped her off a few days ago, my mom had gone shopping for freeze pops, candy, chips, pop and everything else in the "no kids allowed" aisle.

"Thanks mom for keeping her. How was she?"

"A doll as usual. Here's her bag. We went shopping and her grandpa bought her some of the cutest out fits."

"Thank you daddy."

"No problem pumpkin. Anything for granddad's little cupcake." he replied.

We headed home to catch some shuteye before work the next morning. I, of course, had to call Shawntee and tell her about the trip before I retired for the day.

"Glad to see that you guys made it back okay."

"Yeah. We had a ball. The beaches were beautiful."

"Did you do any shopping?"

"I picked up a few things. I got you a t-shirt so remind me to give it to you next time you come by here."

"Did Jeff enjoy himself?"

"Jeff had fun, too. The mosquitoes tore him up but he's okay."

"It's good that you guys had fun and didn't do any arguing."

"Well...we did argue on the plane a little. But we're over it now."

"Try to avoid complications. You two just got back on track."

"I know. Well, I have to work in the morning, so I'll talk to you later."

"I'll probably call you at work tomorrow."

"Okay. Bye."

Shawntee was right. Jeff and I had just put the pieces back together and I didn't want to tear them back down. Jeff was really insecure, and I could see that it was up to me to make this marriage work. It was going to be a tough job, but it was worth it.

I returned to work the next day and walked right in to a big surprise. My boss needed me to leave for Italy in two days. Apparently the young man who filled my previous position couldn't handle it, and they needed someone to go at the last minute. I didn't want to go but I almost didn't have a choice. I was totally committed to my job and gracious for such a big promotion. I could see if they were paying me enough.

"Sure, Rick. No problem. Anything to save the company."

"I knew that you wouldn't leave me hanging. I would go myself, but it's my wedding anniversary and my wife would kill me."

"I understand. You definitely don't want her to knock your head off your shoulders."

"You know how you women are about stuff like this."

"I know. Just leave the itinerary on my desk. I'll call you if I have any questions."

"Can you speak Italian, Rita?"

"Know, but I will in two days. Enough to land this account."

Who in the hell learns a new language in two days? I felt like I was doomed. I wanted to hire a translator, but Rick was funny about spending what he calls "unnecessary" money. I took a trip to the bookstore that evening and purchased some books and tapes. I dreaded telling Jeff about the trip.

"So when do you leave?"

"In two days. I'll only be gone a week."

"If you can get the account in a day, why stay a week. I know your work, Rita. You work hard to land the account the first day, and then you vacation the rest. Can't you just come home after you're done?"

"I have to stay the entire time. I can't just take these folks money and flee. That's not proper business etiquette."

"Are you sure that Rick isn't going with you?"

"Rick never went with me. Why would you ask that?"

Jeff never gave me a response. He just took a deep breath and walked away. I knew that this trip would open a whole can of worms. Jeff was looking to point the blame for something. Anything. I was definitely not trying to give him a reason.

"Welcome to Italy," the stewardess said in so many words. The weather was nice and the people were so friendly. I was ready to take on Italy's corporate world. Just hoped that they were ready for me. I hate to toot my own horn, but I'm a badass sister. When it comes down to business, I don't play. I roll with the best of them.

The driver held a sign with my name on it. I was glad to hear that he spoke English. Actually, I was astonished to find out that a lot of Italians spoke fluent English right there in their native country. I asked the driver if the board members that I was meeting with spoke good English and he said that they did. So I lucked up again.

Now all I had to do was stick to dishes that I recognized and kept close watch over my spending. Foreign exchange could be a headache. Most of my business trips were in the States. I wasn't too trained on how to conduct myself on foreign soil. A lot of beliefs are different and some rituals are unusual. The last thing you want to do is insult or disrespect someone. I read on how Italians conduct business. It was very similar to American ways.

When I met with the company's officials, I found them to be more tolerable than American businessmen. There were impressed that my company sent a woman, and even more impressed that I could hold my own ground. These men were an easy buy due to the fact that they had *roaming eyes*. American women were intriguing to them. Not to say that we're better than Italian women, people just like to see something different.

We're like that in America, too. A lot of people get enticed by a tinted face a unique accent. I don't know what it is but there's something exotic about foreigners. Maybe it's the mystery of not knowing anything about them. The corporate gentlemen that I was dealing with were some type of freaks. They laughed, giggled and made gestures that wouldn't be acceptable in America. If I wanted this account, I had to go along with it. It was acceptable in Italy and unfortunately not labeled as sexual harassment.

It actually took me two days to convince these corporate guru's. I think that the second day was solely for viewing purposes, if you know what I mean. It was cool, though. I was fully aware that my projections weren't the only figures that were impressive. Two days down and two more to go. Shopping was definitely number one on the list.

One of the board members asked me out to dinner which I accepted. Contracts had not yet been signed and I didn't want to chance it. Besides, he was fine and dinner wasn't harmful at all. I called Jeff and Sarah to see what they were up to before I headed out for a night in the town.

"Hey baby. How's everything going?"

"Fine."

"Where's Sarah?"

"Sleep."

"What's be going on?"

"Nothing."

"Why are you giving so many straight answer?"

"I don't have much to say. I'm tired. Some people actually do real work."

"What is that supposed to mean?"

"It means whatever you want it to mean. I have to be at work early tomorrow. Is there anything else?"

"Yeah. I got the account."

"Good for you. Bye."

There was a dial tone afterwards. I could not believe that this chump hung up on me. Jeff wanted to argue and I didn't want to provoke it. The problem is that if I called back, there would be an argument. If I didn't call, there would be one when I got home.

"Why did you hang up on me?"

"I thought that you were done talking."

"No, I wasn't."

"Okay then. What?"

"I told you that I landed the account and you hang up on me?"

"Are you on your way home now?"

"No."

"Why not. You're finished, right?"

"Yeah but I have to stay the full four days. I told you that."

"Well you enjoy yourself, Rita. Is there anything else?"
"I love you."
"Yeah. Bye."

I was growing tired of Jeff's attitude. He wasn't like this in the beginning. It's as if he has turned into a completely different person. I didn't know what to do about him. Maybe we needed counseling.

Dinner was nice and the gentleman took me sightseeing afterwards. The city was striking and I couldn't stop snapping the camera. Antonio was the perfect gentleman the entire night.

"So do you enjoy yourself here in Italy, Rita?"
"Yes. I am having a great time."
"So sad that you can't stay."
"My flight leaves tomorrow evening."

Antonio made a face as if he was sad to see me go. We stopped at a local bar for a couple of drinks. We sipped wine on the patio of the bar and enjoyed each other's company. Antonio walked me back to the hotel where I thanked him for a lovely evening.

"You're welcomed, Rita."
"Next time you're in Italy, call me."

He grabbed me and laid the biggest most romantic kiss on me. It took a couple of seconds for me to realize that it was wrong and that I was a married woman. I hadn't felt passion like that since the first time I kissed Jeff. That was three years ago.

"We can't. I'm married."
"Of course. I apologize. Good night sweet Rita."
"Good night, Antonio. Thanks again for such a lovely evening."
"No problem."

What had I done? It was bad enough that my husband assumed I was cheating. Now this? I felt so guilty and so refreshed at the same time. I must admit that I wanted to make mad passionate love to Antonio. Back in the day, before Jeff's time, I would have. It made me wonder if I sometimes regret marrying Jeff. He initially was just supposed to be a piece of ass. Who knew that he would follow me all the way back to Chicago?

If every man, in every town I've been in followed me home, I'd be on one of those talk shows right now. I honestly missed those days. Traveling was the highlight of my life at that time. I was enjoying my youth and now that was all over. The romance was over and I knew no way of getting it back. No matter how hard I tried, Jeff was pulling further away from me.

There was no Jeff when I arrived at the airport. I called him several times from my cell but there was no answer. My mom hadn't heard from him all day and Shawntee said that when she called there was no answer. He knew what time I was coming in and at what airport. I waited for over an hour before I decided to take a cab home.

I walked in the front door and there was Jeff sitting on the sofa watching television. He never looked up or said a word. I rolled my luggage into the bedroom, which was a pig stein. Sarah was in the crib fast asleep. I sat on the recliner next to Jeff and stared at him in amazement. I couldn't believe that he had no remorse for what he had done.

"So you did this on purpose, huh?"

"Did what?" he asked in a nasty tone.

"Why didn't you pick me up?"

"I thought your little boyfriend, Rick, had arranged a way for you to get home."

"What in the hell is your problem?"

"What's your damn problem? Can't you see I'm trying to watch the game? Shut the fuck up. Damn."

I was at a lost for words. I was fed up with the way Jeff was carrying on. I had never been disrespected by anyone before. The worst of it all is that this wasn't his first time. Jeff had literately cursed me out on several occasions. I had to take a stand now, or accept it throughout the marriage.

"Maybe you're used to talking to women any kind of way, but I'm your wife. Would you accept men talking to your daughter any kind of way?"

"Look, I don't feel like hearing this shit right now. Go sit down somewhere."

"If you're going to be like this from now on, then maybe you don't need to be here."

"So what are you saying?" he asked in rage. "Are you saying that you don't want me here anymore?"

"Not if you're going to continue to disrespect me like this."

"You probably want to move your man up in here. Did Rick finally decide to leave his wife for you?"

"Why do you constantly throw my boss into our arguments? He has nothing to do with this."

"He has a lot to do with it. You think I'm some type of fool don't you?"

"Look, Jeff. I'm getting really tired of your bullshit. You need to get it together or…"

"Or what? You're going to leave me? You don't have to worry about leaving me because I'm getting the hell up out of here."

Jeff stormed out of the front door headed towards his truck. You could smell the rubber burning from his tires. I don't know where he went that night and didn't bother looking for him. Wherever he was, I hoped that he was getting his priorities in order.

I came home from work the next day to dead silence. I could tell that Jeff hadn't been home because nothing in the house had been touched. I waited up for a while before I decided to retire. The next couple of days were long and hectic. I hadn't heard a word from Jeff. He knew that he had accomplished pissing me off, so there was no reason for him to still be gone.

I wanted to call the jails and hospitals but my instincts wouldn't allow me to. Priscilla was even a thought in my mind for a split second, but I felt that he wasn't there either. Where could he be? And with whom? I was too ashamed to tell anyone that he was gone astray. I wasn't in the mood for *I told you so's.*

By the end of week two, I knew that I had to alert someone that Jeff was missing. I was frightened at this point and eager to find my husband. It was almost as if he had pre-planned this whole charade. I decided to inform Shawntee first. I knew that if I called my mom, everyone that she knew would be in my business before the end of the evening.

"It's been days, Shawntee. I don't know where to look for him."

"Did you call the hospitals and jails? Maybe he's at that girl's house again."

"I'm almost certain he's not at those places."

"Maybe he's been camping out at the restaurant all week."

"That factor has been ruled out. He hasn't been to work in days either."

"Did he quit?"

"I don't know. Everyone at the restaurant doesn't know either. They assumed that he was in the hospital and his family just hadn't called yet. Or just an emergency of some sort."

"Does he have any friends in Chicago?"

"Not that I know of. He spends the bulk of his time with us and his co-workers."

"There has to be some place for him to go. Otherwise, he should have come home by now."

"You think, Shawntee?"

"I know that you're frustrated, Rita, and probably tired. Go ahead and call the local hospitals and jails just to definitely rule those out as options. I'm on my way over to help."

I called every hospital, jail and even morgue to find Jeff. He had identification on him, so he should not be a John Doe. A funeral director suggested that I check the John Doe's anyway, in case he had lost his I.D. or been robbed. Shawntee stopped by and we headed out for the funeral homes. Sarah went to my mom's who insisted on knowing what was up.

"Nothing, mother. Shawntee and I are just going out for drinks."

"So why can't Sarah stay home with her dad?"

"He has to work late today."

The last thing I needed was for my mom to stick her nose in my business. Most of the time she means well, but when it comes to men, she's just plain old nosy. It's almost as if she enjoyed when I was lonely, living and traveling alone. She was always happiest when I didn't have a man in my life. She can be a train wreck when it comes to controlling my life. No matter how many up's and down's Jeff and I have, my mom's always going to be there to dictate what I should and shouldn't do or take off of Jeff.

After a long evening of searching for Jeff, Shawntee and I turned in. I didn't bother grabbing the baby because it was so late. I slowly put my key into the door, praying that Jeff would be there. He wasn't. There was a cold stillness in the air. As I entered the bedroom, I was startled to see that someone had been in my house. My immediate thought was that I had been robbed as I grabbed the phone to call the police.

After observing the windows and doors, I realized that I hadn't been robbed after all. In fact, the intruder used no force of entry at all. Jeff had been there, and all of his clothes were gone. I checked the drawers and closet to find that all of his personal belongings had been removed from the house. Even his set of luggage was missing.

It was apparent that Jeff had moved out. He had to have been watching Shawntee and I leaving the house earlier. I was right. This was a plan from the beginning. The act he put on the day that I returned from the trip, his disappearance for days, the missing luggage, was all a part of his plan. He was like a fugitive on the move.

So why did Jeff feel that he had to escape? What was so horrible about being a husband and father? Questions ran through my mind all night. I called Shawntee and she warned me not to blame myself for anything. She was right. It wasn't me with the issues. It wasn't me who ran away from my responsibilities. Jeff was a chump and maybe I was better off without him.

The next morning, I took a sick day from work and went to my mom's to pick up Sarah. My mom had the nastiest look on her face when she answered the door. I knew that I was in for drama. My mom just couldn't let things go when it came to knowing other people's business.

"You lied to me."

"About what?"

"I called Jeff's job last night. He wasn't there. The owner says that he hasn't been there all week and that he was now out of a job. I want to know what in the hell is going on."

"You called his job? You have no right to be calling my husband's job to check up on him."

"I called because I knew that you were lying. Where in the hell were you at last night?"

"It's none of your business. You still had no right to call his job. Do I call your job to see if you're at work or not?"

"This ain't about me. This is about you and your lies. Now dammit, I wan't answers."

"Jeff is gone. He left me and moved out. Are you happy? Now you can have something to discuss at your next block club meeting."

"I knew he wasn't shit. You should have listened to me instead of marrying that bastard. If you can't find him I bet your father can."

"Look. Let me handle my own business. You and daddy just stay out of it."

I grabbed Sarah's hand and left my mother's presence. We went home to dead silence. I cried all night long until my eyes were swollen shut. I knew that I could make it without him financially, but it was a struggle emotionally. No matter where he was, he was still my husband and Sarah's father.

It was hard to go to work and keep a straight face. It was even harder to concentrate on my work. After so long, I knew that I would develop a fake, permanent smile that would hide all of my hurt and pain from the world. O everyone else, I had it all, money, family, and a lovely home. What more could I ask for, huh?

Sarah made it even harder to overcome this situation. She often cries for her daddy and she's not as friendly as she used to be. It was obvious that we were taking a turn for the worse in terms of happiness. I tried to keep Sarah and myself busy by being around others and staying out all day. You can only go to the mall, park and movies so many times.

As the seasons changed and the holidays grew closer, I became more and more weary. I missed my husband and longed to hear from him. I still had no clue as to where he could be and sometimes found myself searching the streets of Chicago for him.

I prayed that he would return soon and that we would be this storybook family. The reality of it all was that he wasn't coming back. It had just been Sarah and I and that was it. That was all it would be for a long time. The holidays were approaching and I knew that I had to get my face together before I stood before members of my family.

All those eyes staring at me were intimidating. I knew that behind the crazy looks were thousands of personal questions waiting to burst out. My father kept his cool during the prayer over Thanksgiving dinner. Unfortunately, my mother had to ruin it in the end.

"In Jesus name, Amen." he ended.

"And God, please let Rita know that this is the time to be by herself for a while. She doesn't need to think about men or even re-marrying for a long time now. She needs to concentrate on raising Sarah. Amen." my mom added.

There was a long silence and then an outburst of laughter from my uncle Charlie. I had never been so embarrassed in my life. How could she stoop so long? My mother had a knack for putting people on the spot. I think what bothered me most was that she meant none of it sincerely. Her sole purpose was to embarrass and make a mockery of me.

Needless to say, I didn't stay at my parent's house for long. Shortly after dinner, I went home so that everyone could have time to talk about me before the night was over. I knew that they were all eager to badger me once I left the premises. It was sure to be an all around *Rita Fest* that Thanksgiving evening.

My family was making a mockery of me; my husband was gone and had no one to stimulate me positively. This seemed to have been the coldest winter ever. I was all alone. There was no one for me to turn to. Even Shawntee had a new man. She spent most of her evenings cuddled up and happy. That was something that I truly missed.

I had made it through one holiday but I broke down at Christmas. Shopping alone, I thought, would be the hardest. Unfortunately there was something worse than tackling the holiday crowds. Christmas morning, I had to watch my baby open her Christmas presents without her daddy. A bastard child at 3, and no clue as to how much of an effect it could have on her.

My parents called to wish her a merry Christmas and that made her day. She still wanted to know where her daddy was, though. I dreaded telling her that daddy's gone. The sad part is that I didn't even have an explanation to give her. It wasn't as if I was lying by omission. Honestly, all I knew is that he was gone.

This was my first time hosting Christmas dinner at my home. Although my family added to my misery, I still wanted them to be close during my time of need. It wasn't money or material things that I needed. What I desired was companionship.

It does me good to hear constant gratitude and praise. Everyone thanked me for such a delicious meal and some praised me for bringing it all together at such a turning point in my life. My mother, of course, wasn't so sincere in her response. She didn't have to try so hard by putting on a fake smile and passing sarcastic compliments.

"Mother, I can do without you patronizing me. How about being happy for me for a change."

"I am happy. Happy that Jeff's gone. Now all you have to do is concentrate on Sarah."

"I'm doing that. But you should know that I'm not going to be alone forever. I will date again. I might even re-marry again. I'm still young."

"You have to get divorced first. Have you looked into that? Or have you just been thinking about hooking up with another man?"

Sometimes it seems as if my mother secretly prayed that I grew up into a lesbian. Even in high school, when I first started dating, she never liked boys around me. Most parents don't, but she was pushier than my dad. Now that I'm an adult, she still hates for me to be with men.

Maybe, it's not about the men at all. Maybe, it's just that she never wanted me to grow up. You would think that she was proud of the woman that I had become. All of the other issues were life problems that she couldn't help me overcome. Once I left the nest that was it. My life was for me to live. My mistakes were for me to make. She made that same transition into adulthood. She should be among the first to understand that it's not about what she wants for me anymore. It's about what I want for myself.

My cousin stayed behind to help me clean up after the guests left. We talked about men, children and family, something we hadn't done since we were kids. I really missed the relationship that we had as children, but our lives were so different now. Our interests weren't merely the same and we've always had a difference of pinions.

Although my family was close, it always seemed somewhat phony to me. We all loved each other very much, but then we get on the phones later and spread each other's business. The only times that we got together as a whole were on holidays. I saw my parents and grandparents at church on Sundays, but that's as far as it went. The rest of them became strangers of some sort.

After putting Sarah to bed, I took a long hot bath and cuddled up to a good movie. This was something I had to get used to during the winter months. I had to find a way to entertain myself and keep my mind off of Jeff. I couldn't spend my whole life dreaming of what might have been.

I nearly choked to death when the phone rang around two in the morning. I was in a deep sleep when the loud rang startled me. My eyes were too blurry to focus on the caller I.D., so I just picked it up and answered it.

"Hello?" I asked.

There was silence so I assumed no one was there. I was about to hang up when I heard a voice from the receiver.

"Rita, don't hang up. It's me, Jeff."

I had awaited this day for months. There was even a prepared speech for when I talked to him. Finally, no words. My hand trembled and tears started to fall from my face.

"Rita, I'm sorry," he continued.

"Jeff where are you? Come home."

"I can't. I can't stay there anymore."

"What did I do?" I asked.

"Nothing. It's me. I wasn't ready, Rita. I wasn't ready to be married or be a father. I should have to you this up front instead of stringing you along all of these years."

"I thought that you loved me."

"I do, Rita, I do. But when I'm with you, I feel less of a man. I feel like you want and deserve to be with someone else. I'm not compatible with you. I'm not good enough for you."

"What about Sarah. You're just giving up on her too?"

"Just because we're not together doesn't mean that I can't be a father to Sarah. Take my number. My phone's about to go dead but I want you to call me later."

"I should have your number on the caller I.D. I'll get it later. I won't be calling you."

"Why not?" he asked.

"Sarah's only three, she can't pick up the phone and call you. It's up to you to develop a relationship with your daughter. I won't be calling on behalf of Sarah. You have to call her yourself."

"That's fair enough. Give her a kiss for me. I'll talk to her soon."

"I love you."

"Bye, Rita."

So that's it? It was obvious that love didn't live here anymore. I knew now that Jeff was just running away from his responsibilities and that I had done nothing to provoke this situation. Even though I was pissed afterwards, the phone call actually shed some light on a few things. I felt as if I was able to go on with my life.

The next morning, I felt a little more refreshed. I now had answers to the questions that pondered in my mind for months. It eased my mind to know that the pain that I had felt wasn't self-inflicted.

Later that evening when I came in from work, I checked the caller I.D to see who had called. A call labeled "Louisiana Call" took me by surprise. I thought for a while and then it came to me when I noticed that the time was marked three o'clock in the morning. Jeff had moved back to New Orleans.

6
BREAD WINNER

So here I am kicking ass and taking names. Who knew that this single mom thing wouldn't be so bad? It was a piece of cake. Sarah was getting bigger and it wasn't as hard as it was when she was a newborn. I had my old life back just with a little sidekick.

Jeff had kept his promise to Sarah by calling her often. I didn't spend much time with friends and family anymore. Shawntee was preoccupied with work, kids and her man. My parents tried to get involved more but I strayed away. This eliminated them out of my personal business.

Overall, I was happy to be free again. There were times that I wanted male companionship, but that problem was soon to be resolved. I was back to my old self and ready to date again. It was a little harder to get back into the dating scene than I had expected. I now had what we all know as baggage. I didn't want to mislead anyone, so I was always honest about me being married but separated. Most men weren't attracted to the fact that I had a child. There was a preconception of baby-daddy-drama.

I later realized that it was easier to tell men that I was separated and my husband now lived in New Orleans. It was even wiser to announce that we were going through a divorce. While this wasn't true, I had to mentally prepare myself for what was bound to happen.

My boss was very pleased with my performance and made me an offer that I couldn't resist.

"Rita, I'm moving to New York to expand our company. I want you to take over this office. I couldn't think of a better person to take over this branch."

"Rick, I'm honored, but would it be permanent or are you just setting up and coming back later."

"No, it's permanent. My wife and I are moving to New York and we want you to run this office. I'll still be the CEO but I'll be more behind the scenes. You can handle it. You're the only other person that knows this business like the back of her hand. What did you think I had been preparing you for all these years."

"I thought that CFO was it for me. Rick, I'm only 29, this is all starting to be surreal."

"Oh it's real. So you better snap back into reality. We have a business to run."

"That's way more of a load to carry."

"Actually, Rita, it's not. You see, all this time, you've been doing my job. I've only been pretending to work hard to make it seem as if there was so much more to the job. So what's become natural to you, is all there is."

"So this is it?"

"Nothing changes but your salary."

At this point, I couldn't handle any more money. I had Benjamin's falling out of my ass. I already didn't know what to do with the money that I currently made. There was only one thing that I could think of. I bought my parents a new home.

"A new home?" my dad started. "What's wrong with this one?"

"Nothing daddy. I just thought that you would like a bigger, better one, in a nicer neighborhood."

"You grew up in this neighborhood."

"Yeah, but things have changed. Besides, you guys spend too much money trying to patch it up."

"That's because it's ours and it's paid for?"

"Let's go see it and maybe you'll change your mind."

We took a long ride to a more quiet, peaceful area. My dad complained that it was too far away. My mom was the only one who knew what the whole idea was.

"So you're trying to get rid of us, huh?"

"That's not it mom."

"Yes it is. But if a new house is the bribe, I'm taking it. When do we move in?"

I knew that my mom wouldn't turn it down. I mean come on, who wouldn't want a new home built from the ground up. Not to mention free. On the ride back. My mom was on her cell phone calling the entire family. She couldn't wait to brag about her new house that her daughter had bought her.

It felt good to be in a position where others benefited from my blessings. I never was the selfish type and always sought to help others in some way. My parents had done so much for Sarah and I, and this was our way of saying 'thank you'.

After buying my parents a new home, everyone had their hands stuck out. So many people wanted money for cars, jewelry, to get out of jail, you name it. These were the many family members who turned their backs when I needed them most. Now the table had turned and everyone needed me. Unfortunately, I couldn't help them. If I offered to help one, I had to help all. I don't recall 'Bank of Rita' being stamped on my forehead.

Jeff was astonishingly pleased with my fortune. Considering that was his so called reason for not being with me, I assumed that he would be bitter.

"I'm proud of you, Rita. There you go, ruling the world again. Just when I think you can't anymore, you always seem to amaze me."

"Well I do what I can."

"And so modest, too."

"You want to talk to Sarah?"

"Sure. Put her on the phone."

I knew that it was best that I didn't talk with Jeff long. I didn't want to mislead him and make him think that I was still in mourning over him. Sometimes he would ask if I was seeing anyone or if I had started dating again. Not once has he mentioned divorce. I didn't make any suggestions either. I wanted to wait and see what his next move would be.

He talked to Sarah a while and then asked to speak to me again. I felt the conversation leading into something else, so I backed out and wished him a good evening.

"You have a good evening, too, Rita. I love you."

There was a pause and then a dial tone. I couldn't believe that he had dug that one up. As many times as I have said those words, he should have been said something. The phone rang back, but I didn't answer. I wasn't in the mood for playing mind games with Jeff.

Why is it that when times get tough, men tend to back out and run away? And once you patch things back up, they come running back. Why can't most me mend the pieces themselves? I was tired of picking up the pieces. Hell, I could just buy new ones.

I was looking fabulous at my parents house warming. People complimented me on how revived I looked. Some even commented on how well I bounced back after the whole "Jeff" incident. It was obvious that didn't need a man to complete me. I was whole before I met him.

The house warming was a success and my parents had done a great job with the decorating. Their living room furniture was so old that it had gone out of style and came back. Once she took the plastic off, it was like all new furniture.

"The place looks nice mom. You and dad really outdid yourselves."

"Thanks, baby. We were able to spend from our savings and purchase some new items. Your dad was always a great painter so of course he had to show off on these new walls."

"The colors are very vibrant. You two must have been watching some of those home decorating shows."

"That was the only way for us to get hip to today's fashion."

I hated when my mom tried to talk cool. She was always way off. Sometimes, I wished that she would just enjoy being herself and appreciated getting older. My dad never tried to fit in. He was always old-fashioned and set in his ways.

During the dinner, my dad pulled me to the side. He said that he needed to talk with me in private. It startled me because I thought that he had some life-threatening secret to tell me.

"I talked to Jeff this morning. He wants to come home."

"He called you? Why?"

"He's sorry, Rita and he want you back."

"Not a chance. I'm happy and I don't choose to go back to the verbal abuse."

"Verbal abuse?"

"I never told you, but Jeff used to curse me head-to-toe, daddy. Ha talked to me like I was a dog."

"I didn't know that it was that bad."

"Of course you didn't. It's a lot of stuff that you and mom don't know."

"Well I promise that I won't share this with your mother. This is your business. You don't need her sticking her big fat nose in it."

"Thank you daddy."

"You should still consider taking him back. I was Jeff once. He's confused and intimidated by your success. A lot of men don't know how to handle strong women. You can be a handful, you know?"

"I guess you're right. I'll think about it."

"Well whatever you decide, I'm behind you one hundred and ten percent."

"Thanks dad."

It was good that I could talk to my dad without my mom being around. When I was younger, my dad would sneak me to the movies when my mom said "No". My dad was my best friend and I knew that I could count on him to keep my mom out of my business.

I couldn't believe that Jeff had called my father. I must admit that I was impressed. I wonder if everything weren't going so well, would Jeff still want me back. Sometimes, men can't stand for you to be happy without them. That's why they try to come back after they've left you. Now don't get me wrong, there's a handful that actually comes back because they truly love and miss you. But honestly, most of it is misery.

People always want to believe that the grass is greener on the other side, but it's not. It's the same damn color. Sometimes it's even yellow and starting to die. This was something that Jeff had to learn. The lesson that he was learning was the lesson of life. Things don't come easy in this world. You have to work for what you want. If I was what Jeff wanted, he had to put in some work.

Being back in the dating scene really opened my eyes to some things. All the men that I dated were the same. Most men would complain that I was just picking the "wrong men", but that wasn't it. All men do the same things as do all women. The difference is that our actions are carried out at different times and different stages in our lives.

This imbalance of activities is what makes us all different. There are good men out there that have never cheated on a woman. Most likely, there was a time where they did cheat and just grew out of it, or that they never did cheat and will grow into it. Maybe there are even a small percentage of men that miss out and happen to die before it happens. Who's to say that if they continued to live, they wouldn't cheat? Sounds crazy but it applies to women too.

Nobody's perfect. We all have done some things to inflict pain on another being. Forgiveness is the key in it all. It's easier to blame someone than it is to forgive him or her. I I blamed Jeff for so much. Hell, I even started blaming him for things that occurred on the job. I was hurt and upset. I was down right pissed off and I wanted him to beg.

I had a date one Friday with this musician. I had heard him play at a jazz restaurant one evening. We talked a while and he invited me back for dinner.

"I couldn't help but notice you in that teal dress that evening." he started.

"I couldn't help but notice that you knew that it was teal."

"I have three sisters. I know all about fashion, hair care and shopping."

"The key essentials." I responded.

We enjoyed a dry, white wine while we listened to some smooth jazz. Carl, the musician, was cute but he wasn't rub up against me fine. He seemed very intelligent, though. He carried a conversation well. Everything was going okay until I asked the question of the day.

"Well you say that you're not married and has never been married. Do you have ay children?"

"Yes." he responded. "Five."

I laughed until I realized that he had made a serious gesture. Suddenly, it wasn't funny anymore. Instantly, he wasn't interesting anymore. I continued the dinner in respect for him paying. At the end of the evening, I shook his hand and wished him a good night.

"You're never going to call me again are you?" he asked.

"No. I'm sorry."

"Don't be. I always get that reaction when I tell women how many kids I have. Good day, Rita."

"Good day."

What? I know that you didn't expect me to stick around. Oh yeah, like any of you want the brother with five kids and four baby mommas. Not me! I already had enough drama in my life. I could do without someone else's.

This dating business was about to be over for me. I was considering throwing in the towel. There was something wrong with every man that I dated. If they didn't live with someone: momma, a friend, a woman, they were unemployed and without a car. I couldn't find anyone that wasn't married and compatible. I know it's a double standard considering I am married, but my husband and I are separated. Truth of the matter is, we weren't legally separated and that made me just as bogus as the men I dated.

One night I decided to give Jeff a call at the number on my caller I.D. Someone else answered and told me that that number was to a pay phone. I didn't understand what was going on. Why was Jeff calling from a pay phone? I attempted to call his cell phone, but just as I predicted, it was off.

Another day went by and I finally heard from Jeff. He had called from the same number as usual. It was strange how he was able to block out the background noise. I wanted to know what was up.

"Jeff, where are you?"

"New Orleans. I told you that."

"No. Where are you calling me from?"

"Home."

"Where do you live?" I asked.

"I'm back at my friend's house."

"Jeff, I tried to call this number earlier, you didn't answer."

"That's because we weren't home. My friend doesn't have voice mail."

"Someone did answer."

"They did?" he asked surprisingly.

"Yeah, and they said that it was a pay phone."

"My boy was probably just playing on the phone."

"What's going on Jeff? Tell me the truth."

He went on to tell me how he was staying with a friend who ended up moving out of town a month later. He wasn't working, so he was unable to pay the rent.

"I got evicted and I've been living in a shelter for months now."

"Why didn't you go to a family member's house?"

"You know how that goes. They're already pissed at me because I married you and moved to Chicago. They don't want to have anything to do with me."

"Why didn't you say anything to me?"

"I was ashamed. I've done so much to you already, Rita, I couldn't dare ask to come home."

As bad as I wanted to leave his broke ass down there, I couldn't. He was my husband and I loved him. In sickness and in health, 'til death do us part? He wasn't dead yet, and I made a vow to God that I would stand by him.

"Do you want to come home Jeff?"

"Yes. More than anything."

"Will you get your act together?"

"I promise."

I wired Jeff some money so that he could get home. I was excited and sad at the same time. I was eager to see my husband, but embarrassed that I was caving in. Here I go again playing some supernatural hero. I could only pray that things were about to change.

Sarah and I dressed in our best out fits. I wanted to look good for my man. Not to mention that I hadn't had sex in a little over a year. I was horny and ready to tear the bedroom up. I told Sarah that we were going to see daddy and there was no response. She wasn't as excited as I thought she would be. In fact, she showed no emotion at all.

Was Sarah going through daddy withdrawal? I guess when you're young; it's easy to erase someone from your memory. I assumed that all this time she spent talking to him was void. For her, it was like talking to a stranger. She knew who her daddy was and still called him daddy, but there was no relation for her at all.

I walked across the terminal in search for Jeff. We were late picking him up due to stormy weather. I felt a tug at my shirt and was startled by the strange man behind me. It was Jeff. I had walked right past him and didn't recognize him.

"Hey baby. Come here and give daddy a hug."

He picked Sarah up for a kiss and she pushed away. He looked as if he had been stranded in the mountains for years. His hair was long on his head, and braided to the back. He had stubble all over his face and he smelled of alcohol.

"Have you been drinking?"

"A little. I had a couple of drinks on the plane."

"When's the last time you took a bath?"

"Are you going to patronize me or kiss me?"

"I'm certainly not kissing you with that rat on your face and liquor on your breath. We're stopping by the barber's."

It may have been storming, but I was determined to turn my frog into a prince. We stopped at the barber's along the way and I waited patiently for them to transform him. They frowned at the thought of touching him. I don't care how bad he smelled, they had to turn old Moses into Jesus.

The haircut and trim was better, but he still wasn't kissable. I ran his bath water while he played with Sarah. He wanted me to join him, but I couldn't. I hated the smell of a drunk.

"Don't forget to brush and gargle, too. Repeatedly."

"Damn baby. I'm that bad?"

"Worse."

I slipped into my sexiest lingerie in hopes that he would arouse me after a good bath. Sarah was fast asleep in her bed and the rain set the mood for the evening. I cracked a window and lit a few candles around the room. I laid on the bed and posed for my man.

It was obvious that Jeff was immediately aroused as he entered the room. He proceeded to throw his clothes in the hamper but I redirected him to the garbage. Everything in his hands were soiled and had to be disposed of. I knew that the man underneath all of that filth was my Jeff, and I was right.

Being homeless must have had a big effect on Jeff's sexual drive. Who knows? Maybe it was I. Maybe I was just horny as hell. All I know is that that was the best sex that Jeff had ever given me. The passion was so strong that night.

"Rita, I really missed you and I'm sorry for all of the pain that I've inflicted on you. I really do love you and want to spend the rest of my life with you."

"So, honestly, why did you leave?"

"It's not you, it's me. I have some personal issues. I would try to explain, but it's complicated."

"I'm your wife. What's so complicated that you can't tell me?"

"I just have to get my shit in order, that's all. I may not be the man that you want me to be, but I am a man. Just be a little patient as I get it together, Rita."

I was willing to be patient, but unwilling to let Jeff walk all over me again. I loved him dearly and it was obvious that he needed me at such a critical point in his life. We spent the evening discussing how we were going to fix this problem. Jeff seemed sincere about getting it together. I could only hope that he was,

One of the first things that Jeff had to do was find a new job. I'm sure that Palagios' wasn't interested in hiring him back. It was going to be hard but he had to get back out there and try.

"So you're job hunting today, right?"

"Yeah. My suits are still in the closet, right?"

"No. You took everything with you. You don't have a suit?"

"Not unless there's one hiding around here somewhere."

"Here. Take this money and get up and buy a suit. You'll still have time to job hunt is you get up now. I have to get to work. Love you."

"Love you too, honey. Have a good day at work."

Jeff almost ruined his work history by deserting his last job. I insisted that he never mentioned Palagios' to a prospective employer and act as if this was his first time in Chicago. He didn't want to go that route and thought that it would be helpful to explain the situation. I was from the Chi, and I knew that these people didn't want to hear shit.

I had a feeling that Jeff's day wouldn't go according to plan. When I got home that evening, Jeff was sitting on his ass with a pile of garbage sitting around him. You could tell that he had been sitting in the same spot all day.

"How was your job search today?"

"Dead. Everyone say that they're not hiring. Some wouldn't even accept my resume."

"Where's the suit that you bought?"

"I didn't buy a suit. I'll get one tomorrow."

"So what did you wear?"

"This."

I could not believe that Jeff went job-hunting "as is". He looked as if he hadn't showered, brushed his teeth, or washed his face. His clothes looked like something that he got out of the dirty clothes hamper. He proceeded to clean up the mess that lurked around my sofa.

After making dinner, I made a couple of phone calls. During my lunch break, I stopped to talk to two restaurant owners that I was very well acquainted with. Upon talking to one of them, I was able to land Jeff an interview.

"Jeff. Here's the address to Tony's Italian Restaurant. You have an interview with the owner on Friday. Please be on time. This is a favor from a friend."

"Thanks but no thanks. I'm a grown ass man, Rita. I don't need for you to find a job for me."

"I'm just trying to help. You need a job and I'm not gonna have you sitting around the house all day."

"I said that I'd get one. I don't need your help. Who is this guy anyway? Why does he owe you any favors?"

"He doesn't owe me anything. He's a good friend of mind."

"Yeah right, good friend. How come I never met this so called friend? So you met him while I was away?"

"No. I used to have lunch at his restaurant. I've known him for years. Are you going or what?"

"I'll think about it."

I had a gut feeling that Jeff wasn't going. Don't you hate it when someone does you a favor and another person has to mess it up? He was intentionally trying to ruin my reputation with my friend.

Weeks went by and Jeff had an excuse for everything. My house was a mess everyday and his laundry was limited. He had gotten into the habit of wearing the same thing everyday.

"I'm in the house," he would say. "Why do I have to change clothes? That's a waste of an outfit."

"If you went out and looked for a job, you wouldn't be wearing the same thing everyday."

There was a moment of silence. Jeff didn't respond after that. It was obvious that Jeff didn't plan on working. He wanted me to take full responsibility of being the breadwinner.

I can't say that I wasn't pleased with having a lazy ass househusband. I continued to push for Jeff to find a job, but he wouldn't. Jeff had developed a lazy persona and he was planning on sticking to it.

Surprisingly, I called home during lunch one day and Jeff wasn't there. I was glad to see that he had come to his senses and went out to look for a jab. On the way home, I stopped by the bakery to grab a cake. Sometimes you have to treat men like children and reward their efforts.

I walked in to find Jeff fast asleep that evening. I leaned in to kiss him when I noticed a smudge of lipstick on his collar. My initial reaction was to smack him on the back of his head. Instead, I let him rest. Sounds crazy, but I wasn't about to jump to conclusions. If Jeff were up to no good, it would all come to light sooner or later.

Jeff awoke from his nap when he heard Sarah laughing and playing in the living room. He picked her up and bought her in the kitchen where I was fixing dinner.

"Hey baby. How was your nap?"

"Good. I had gotten out early today and I was dead tired when I got in."

"How was your day?' I inquired.

"Busy. Things are looking good though. I've got interviews lined up for the next couple of days."

One thing that I hate is a liar. If you'll lie, you'll steal. If you'll steal, you'll kill. Jeff was killing me with that lame ass story that he made up. Above all, I still didn't burst him out. I just played along. I hadn't collected enough evidence yet anyway.

As time went by, Jeff went on more and more interviews, but there was till no job. I had mentally prepared myself to catch him cheating. This time around, I decided to lay low. I didn't have the time or energy to play private investigator.

"Jeff have you considered any position other than restaurant manager?"

"It's all that I know. There's nothing more for me to do."

"I just think that you should consider something else until another management position comes along. A lot of these prestigious restaurants have managers who've held their positions for years. It may be a while before something comes along."

"Well I'll just have to wait. I'm not flipping burgers and dropping fries."

"I'm not suggesting that, I just think that you should try something for the time being."

"Don't worry, Rita. Something will come along sooner or later and you won't have to worry about me just sitting around anymore."

Jeff walked out with an attitude. After everything that I had done for him, he still hadn't changed. He was so ungrateful. You wouldn't have known that he was homeless just months ago.

I was tired of taking care of Jeff, and even more tired of trying to turn him into a man. Bottom line, Jeff just didn't want tot do right. He was determined to live off of me and enjoy his freedom all at the same time. I was responsible for all of the bills, his and mine. I already got him out of debt once, how did he fall back in so fast?

Apparently Jeff had credit cards that he couldn't pay off. I don't know what he was charging, but whatever it was, it wasn't coming into our home. He even had an overdrawn bank account that I was just now finding out about. I wouldn't be surprised if the IRS was on his tail. Without a doubt, Jeff was the king of scams.

Needless to say, Jeff was soon to be anchored to my sofa if I didn't put my foot down. He knew that I wasn't going to put him out. Some of you may say, "Leave his ass!" but I'm sure you guys aren't married. When you want a marriage to work, it's not so simple. Hey, love is war, baby!

7
UNEXPECTED SITUATIONS

Everything that we claim we wouldn't accept when we're single is the first thing that we accept when we're married. People can seem so perfect when you're dating them, but once you're married, they become hazardous to your health. Case and point.... Jeff. I've never suffered migraines until recently.

It's a bad feeling when you come home and your man's sitting in the same exact spot that he was sitting in when you left him that morning. It boiled my butt everyday to find my husband slain in the slop that he created. My grocery bill seemed to have been climbing higher everyday. True enough he wasn't hurting my pockets, but honestly, what woman wants to take care of her man? I could have sworn that men were supposed to be the heads of households.

Jeff hadn't searched for a job in months now. He constantly blamed his lack of employment on the weather.

"Winter I Chicago is no joke, baby. I'm having a hard time adjusting to this weather."

"Jeff, you're in the car. Turn the damn heat on."

"I still have to sit in the car while it warms up. I could freeze to death. You know that I'm anemic."

"Just admit that you're lazy and don't want to work."

"I do want to work, baby. I'll start back looking as soon as the weather breaks."

Winter weather doesn't break until May in Chicago. It's always cold here. Let's face it. I had a deadbeat, good for nothing, lazy ass husband. Unfortunately, I wouldn't trade him for the world. Hell, no one else would want him anyway.

I noticed a lot of Louisiana calls on my bill one day. When I confronted Jeff about them, he came up with another on of his fabulous lies.

"My parents and I are talking again. We hooked back up when I was back home."

"If you guys were such a family again, why didn't they offer you a place to stay?"

"They didn't know that I was homeless. I didn't want to impose."

It was apparent that Jeff was lying, seeing as though we never had incoming calls from New Orleans. It's been going on five years now and not once have I met Jeff's parents. I was tempted to dial the number and confront his family, but I didn't want to start any shit. I knew that by calling the numbers, I would be opening up a whole can of worms.

By not knowing Jeff's family, there was a gap in our relationship. His family was a whole part of him that was a secret. It was almost as if they didn't exist. I knew nothing of Jeff's history other than what he told me. Being the liar that he was, I wouldn't be surprised if his whole life was a lie.

My fairytale had indefinitely turned into a nightmare. The man that I thought I was marrying turned out to be a fluke. Myself? I was everything that I was supposed to be. There were no hidden fees behind this credit application. If I may say so myself, I've soared above and beyond Jeff's expectations. Above all, I was doomed. I didn't think that thinks could get any worse than they already were.

I scooped Sarah up from preschool one afternoon only to discover a disturbed look on her teacher's face. Apparently, Sarah had been anti-social and inactive all day. Her teacher said that she just wasn't herself that day.

"She's been a bit peculiar Mrs. Bridges. Is everything okay at home?"

"Everything's fine. What has she been doing?"

"Sitting in the corner all day."

"You put her in time out?"

"No. Not at all. Around nap time, she climbed out of her cot and just went straight to the corner and started rocking."

"Has she been in the Indian position all day?"

"Ever since nap time."

I couldn't pin point what the problem was right then and there. I informed her teacher that I would talk to Sarah and deal with the situation at home. When I reached down to pick Sarah up, she put her hands over her ears and started screaming to the top of her lungs.

What could have triggered this unusual behavior? I was certain that it had something to do with her father's return. When I finally got her in the car seat, she calmed down. The constant rocking hadn't ceased. I wasn't sure if the teacher had done something, or if Sarah was having behavioral problems.

I felt that it would be wise to wait a day and monitor Sarah's behavior. She went to school but I checked on her repeatedly during the course of the day. Sure enough, at naptime, there was Sarah, nestled in the corner, away from everyone. She wasn't rocking because she was actually sleep this time.

At the end of the day, Sarah's report wasn't positive. It appears that something dramatic had happened to Sarah.

"What did you do to her?" I asked the teacher. "She was fine when I dropped her off yesterday."

"Mrs. Bridges, we didn't do anything. You can ask the kids. When I yelled naptime, Sarah climbed onto her cot like everyone else. During the course of her nap, she woke up and went straight for the corner."

"Why didn't you come and get me?"

"Well I didn't think that there was anything wrong at first. But then I tried to pick her up and she went into a temper tantrum."

"Did any of the kids say or do anything to her?"

"No. I was sitting here the whole time."

"I wasn't sure who to blame, but I was certain to find out what had happened to my daughter. I took her to the pediatrician that day and they decided to run some tests on her. I didn't know what these tests were for, but I noticed the doctor consulting her colleagues.

The physician beckoned for me to come into her office. I was taken by the disdained look on her face. I was not prepared for what the doctor told me.

"Mrs. Bridges, Sarah is autistic."

"What?"

"It's nothing hereditary and no one in her class, including the teacher, caused this."

"She wasn't born this way. I don't understand. How could this just happen?"

"That's the tricky thing about autism. Most children don't develop it until their preschool years. Your child's normal today, and the next day, you find them in the corner facing the wall or talking to themselves. The behavior varies with each case."

My heart sank as the physician proceeded to explain my child's situation. I had so many questions. I knew that taking care of her would be a much harder task. The news was devastating and I was afraid of how our lives were going to pan out.

Later that night, Jeff and I cried as we watched Sarah doze off to sleep. Not only did I have the new issue to deal with, I still had this asshole in my life. I couldn't help but wander what the hell he was crying for. I mean, come on, it's not like he was in a position to help me with Sarah.

I called my mother and attempted to explain everything without choking up. It was almost impossible. My mother cried with me a while and then she let her strong side shine through.

"Rita, baby. It's going to be okay. God will put no more on you than you can bear."

"But what did I do wrong, mom?" I asked in a high-pitched, squeaky voice. "Maybe it's not me. Maybe it's Jeff. All of the drama in the house probably traumatized my baby."

"As much as we'd love to point the blame, we can't. It's neither one of your faults."

"It's going to be so hard now, mom. It's not like I can really depend on Jeff."

"Well you've got me and your dad. We'll help until you get in the swing of things."

Get in the swing of things? I didn't even know where to start. What about school? What about work? Lord, why me? Every time I thought it couldn't get any worse, it did. I felt like I had hit rock bottom.

Ever feel like you just can't go on anymore, but somehow, you dig up enough faith, courage and strength to do so? Whoever said, "A woman's work is never done", wasn't lying. We go on because we don't have a choice. Real women don't have options, we have duties. Everything is a must for us.

I prayed and prayed day in and day out. My boss allowed me a week off to figure out how I was going to tackle this issue. I wasn't comfortable with putting Sarah in a special school, yet. Taking her to work everyday was out of the question.

My boss, Rick, came to my house one evening to see how I was doing. This came as a surprise because he had never come to my home before. Luckily, Jeff was there so he shouldn't have had a reason to make assumptions. Rick had met Jeff before and could sense that Jeff felt inferior around him. This was an embarrassment, knowing that my husband was a punk.

"So have you decided what you wanted to do with Sarah, yet?" Rick asked.

"No, not yet. It's such a big dilemma. I don't know what to do. I don't even know my options, if I have any."

"I was thinking…it's not like your presence is needed at the office. We only need you to check in every now and then. You've always been better off working alone anyway."

"What are you saying?"

"I'm saying that you might be able to work from home. I've conducted a few satellite conferences in the past and the results were astounding."

"Yeah? I could set up my office right here."

"Exactly. All you need is a fax machine and a satellite system and you're good to go. Although, you're still required to check in twice a week. You wouldn't have to stay long. You can take Sarah with you."

I was so overjoyed that I immediately hugged Rick and burst into tears. I was so grateful that I had a concerned and helpful boss. I was even more grateful that I was able to keep my job. With Jeff being out of work for so long, losing my job would have been like diving flat onto a body of water. Fortunately, God saved me from that belly flop.

Rick and I wrapped up our conversation as I walked him to his car. I could see Jeff peering out of the blinds from upstairs.

"Rick you've done so much for me and my family. How could I ever repay you?"

"Keep raising those figures that's all. Rita you're the best thing that ever happened to Candy Records. Without you, my company may have crashed years ago."

"Well, I guess I'll see you tomorrow."

"I'll be here with your equipment and office supplies."

Once again, I gave Rick a big tight squeeze and then I let him go about his evening. I was so surprised that he flew into Chicago, just to check on me. Jeff, on the other hand, was not so thoughtful and concerned. Hmm…made me wonder what his true feelings were towards his own daughter.

"You and your boss sure are friendly. Do you hug all of your co-workers like that?" Jeff started as I shut the front door.

"Jeff, this is the wrong time for this shit. Our daughter has an illness that cannot be cured and the only thing you're concerned about is my boss and I. I could have lost my job. Everything is at stake right now."

"You can't lose your job when you're screwing the boss."

Jeff snatched his coat and once again, stormed out of the front door. This time, I didn't attempt to go after him. I almost wanted him to just disappear, never come back. I should have left his ass where I found him.

After all the rage, I looked up and there was Sarah, bright eyed and bushy tailed. The last thing she needed to see was mommy and daddy arguing. I picked her up and turned on the television. She laid her head on my chest, and for that moment, everything was okay.

A few weeks had gone by and I was getting the hang of things. Sarah's behavioral patterns were becoming familiar and unfortunately, so were Jeff's. Sarah only rocked when she sat in one spot, like in front of the television, or at the dinner table. Sometimes, she would say the same things twice, like an echo. Her learning skills were strong in some areas and weak in others. She didn't want people outside of the family to touch her. If Sarah hadn't developed a relationship with you, she kicked and screamed if you attempted to touch her. Funny thing about it all; she wouldn't let Jeff touch her.

Jeff's behavioral routine, on the other hand, became familiar. I noticed that he hated that I was home everyday. It was as if he was allergic to Sarah and I. He started hanging out in taverns during the day and sleeping through the night. Our relationship had faltered and sex was non-existent. I had too much on my plate. There was no time for me to cater to Jeff.

"Wake up. Wake your ass up." Jeff yelled, interrupting my sleep.

"Jeff go away. You've been out drinking again. I don't have time for this. I'm tired."

"Wake up." he insisted. "You're gonna make love to me tonight."

"No. You're drunk."

Jeff forced himself on top of me and proceeded to pull down my underwear. I was wearing a nightgown so it was hard for me to keep myself covered while I wrestled with him. Eventually, my panties ripped and Jeff was forced inside of me.

"Jeff, I said no."

"Bitch, you're my wife. There's no such thing as 'No'."

I wanted to scream, but I knew that no one would come. He was so rough and violent, that I couldn't help but pound and scratch for him to get off of me. He even pulled my hair and put his hands on my throat once or twice.

When he finally stopped, my body laid limp while I gasped for air. I thought that he was going to choke me to death. He stared down at me in rage while he pulled up his slacks. Just when I thought it was over, it happened. He puked all over me, wiped his mouth, and rolled over for bed.

I felt like shit. Better yet, I felt like the puke that came out of his mouth. As I climbed into the shower, the hot water burned my tears and rips. I cried in that shower for over two hours. The more I washed, the filthier I felt. I knew then, that sooner or later, this marriage would become the death of me.

I was too humiliated to tell anyone. Jeff walked around everyday, as if nothing ever happened. If only I had known that that night was a night of many. Jeff said that he was being sexually neglected and that I had to give him sex on call. Shamefully, I did.

I feared for Sarah more so than myself. I was afraid that she would grow up and he may beat or rape her. I didn't want Jeff near her, and he seemed perfectly fine with that.

"Fine. I didn't want to be bothered with her retarded ass anyway," he said one evening.

"You son-of -a-bitch. Get out of my house."

"Gladly." Jeff put his keys on the coffee table and left right out.

"No. I don't think you understand. I want you out of our lives forever."

"Bitch please. This is my house. I bought you this house. Remember?"

"Yeah I remember. Stay away from us or I'll have you arrested. Remember that!"

Jeff left that night and didn't return. His actions were interfering with my work, and ruining my life. I can't say that I felt safer with or without him. I was confused. Shawntee came by to surprise me and I had to lie to save face.

"Where's Jeff?" she asked.

"He's out job hunting today. Hard to believe huh?"

"Yeah. Hard to believe." Shawntee gave a fake laugh as if she knew that I was lying.

"Hey Shawn. Hey Shawn." Sarah yelled from her bedroom. She came into the living room and sat next to Shawntee.

"Hey Sarah. What's going on big girl?"

"The wheels on the bus go round and round." Sarah sang. Then she burst into laughter.

"I see Sarah's doing pretty well."

"Yeah." I continued. "I've been working with her. She has her moments though."

"And Jeff? Is he helping at all?"

"Oh yes. He's wonderful."

"You liar."

"What?" I asked.

"You're hiding something. What is it?"

"It's nothing."

"Ah hah. So you admit there is an it and that it may be something."

"What? You're not making any sense. I wonder about you sometimes."

"All I'm saying is that if there was something, you'd tell me right?

"Right."

"Good. Now let's go shopping."

"I'm really not in the mood for shopping, Shawntee."

"Not in the mood? How dare you say such bad things in front of Sarah like that? Right Sarah?"

"Right Shawn. That's right. Right." Sarah responded.

Shawntee always knew how to cheer me up. Since Sarah was diagnosed, I had been secluded to my house. My mom came by a few times but I tried to keep her away. I knew that it wouldn't be long before the bloodhounds sniffed out my business.

For the first time ever, I had gone into a mall and didn't know what to buy. I hadn't left the house in so long that there was almost no need for new clothes. I ended up purchasing some things for Sarah. I even bought a blouse for my mother.

"Girl, what's wrong? I know you ain't broke."

"No. Of course not. I'm not in a big shopping mood. There's nothing more for me to buy anyway. I already have a closet full of clothes; most of which still have the tags on them."

"So what do you do with all of your money?"

"Pay bills."

"You know what I mean, Rita. Even after you pay bills, you still have a lot of money left over."

"I have shares of stock and I've invested some money into a couple of small businesses. I even donate a portion of my salary to charities and non-profits. You know; big tax write off at the end of the year."

"So with your reinvestments, I'm sure that you're bringing in far more cheddar."

"If by cheddar you mean money, then yes. I bring in a lot of cheddar."

"So I'm saying…Can a sister get a loan? Better yet, call it a girlfriend grant. This way I don't have to pay you back."

Shawntee was the last person on Earth who would honestly ask me for money. Needless to say, in her time of need, Shawntee could call me for anything. I would give her my last.

Sometimes, I wished that anyone other than Jeff would ask me for money. I would feel better giving it to someone with a job. Someone who would actually be in a position to pay me back.

I came home with take-out, but Jeff had already prepared a candlelight dinner. I must admit that I hadn't expected him back so soon. The smile on his face made me afraid to eat.

"What's the occasion, sweetie?"

"Let's eat first and then I'll tell you the big surprise."

It was wiser for him to go ahead and tell me first. Hell, for all I knew, the big surprise could have been my death. I waited until he took a few bites. Even then I was still afraid to eat.

"Why aren't you eating, Rita?"

"My food's cold. Can you fix me another plate?"

"You can just put that one in the microwave."

"You know that I hate to reheat my food."

"Alright. Alright."

I observed Jeff as he put my plate on the counter and fixed me a new one. Sarah was busy eating her take-out, so she was on the safe-side. I didn't know what Jeff was up to, but I sure was suspicious.

"Here you go, honey", he said as he put my plate on the table.

"Hmm. Smells good."

"Eat up. So we can get to the good news."

"You know what honey. Why don't we just cut straight to the good news now."

"Okay. Guess what?"

"What?"

"I got a new job."

"Bullshit."

"No kidding. I took your advice and I'm stepping outside of the restaurant business. Just temporarily though."

"So what are you going to be doing?"

"Bartending down at this new club that I've been hanging out at."

"So this is a night job?"

"Yeah. What does it matter? It's a job."

Can't say that I was thrilled at all. I knew in the back of my mind, the real reasons why Jeff wanted this job. Being a bartender meant that he could have access to all of the free drinks (and women) that he wanted. Best of all, he didn't have to come home to me at night.

"Yeah. I'll be working seven to three in the morning."

"I'm sure."

"What's wrong? I thought you'd be thrilled about my new job."

"I am. Don't you see me turning flips?"

The only good thing about this situation is that Jeff wouldn't be in my hair anymore. I guess it's even a good thing that he'll soon find someone to fulfill his sexual desires. Sounds crazy, but you'd feel the same way if someone imposed unwanted sex on you every night.

It was only a matter of time before Jeff was in the swing of things. His new uniform of tight jeans and t-shirts made him look like his old self again. I watched him prep for all the drunken, loose women. He would slick his hair with wave grease and bathe in cologne. It even took him three to four minutes to grease his lips.

"You look nice, honey." I complimented.

"Thanks."

He grabbed his leather jacket and paraded out the door. There was nothing left but silence. Sarah was sleep, and there I was: tired, bored and lonely. The nightlife didn't exist for me. I lived through the stories and experiences of Jeff. Sometimes he would tell me about guest appearances and bar fights. This would become the most excitement that I would encounter for the next couple of months, maybe years.

Life as I knew it was over for me. I had come to the conclusion that I was put on this Earth to take care of others. When the time comes, who's going to take care of me? Sarah can't do it. My parents would be too old, or dead. Jeff might even try to kill me before my time.

The phone rang in the middle of the night, waking Sarah and myself. It was Jeff, lying about how he had to stay a little later. You could hear the women giggling in the background.

"So what time do you think you're going to be home Jeff?"

"Around five thirty, six o'clock."

That's the next morning. He might as well have stayed whoever the hell he was. See that's what really burns my butt. If these women can sleep with you and turn all types of tricks every night, why can't they offer you a place to stay? As soon as you tell a brother to get the hell out, all of a sudden they don't have any place to go.

It amazes me how men can all of a sudden get jobs when they don't want to be around you. Jeff was content with sitting at home, unemployed, as long as I was at work and out of his face. True enough, some men would just leave you, but most men don't have the balls to do so. Instead, they introduce infidelity and drama into our lives and expect us to just accept it.

The next morning, Jeff stumbled in, reeking of alcohol, perfume and sex. Just looking at him made me want to sanitize the entire house. The worse thing of it all is that Jeff knows that I'm aware of what's going on and he doesn't even care.

"What are you looking at me so crazy for?"

"You stink." I replied.

"So does your morning breath. Get out of my face."

"Make sure that you bathe before climbing your nasty ass into my bed."

I could hear Sarah moving around in her bedroom. I hated that she had to constantly hear our bickering. I was afraid that it might worsen her condition in some way. She never showed emotion towards the arguing. Most kids act out by slamming their doors, crying, or yelling back at their parents. From Sarah.... there was nothing. Hmm. Made me wonder what was really going on in her genius little head.

What amazed me most about Sarah was that she knew things that a normal preschooler wouldn't. On the contraire, she didn't know the things that were familiar for her age group. Just from watching television, Sarah could tell me all about forensic science or about different types of spiders and the regions that they live in. She couldn't tell you about the Itsy Bitsy Spider, though. The song, and species, was unknown to her.

I would take her to the parks and she would charm the elderly by identifying their dogs and what breed they were. People were astonished by her intelligence. If only they knew that she didn't even know her ABC's anymore. It's almost as if her though pattern had been rearranged. It made me wonder if that may somehow reverse, as she got older.

Time went on and each day I started to wonder if it was the day that I would wake up from this nightmare. At the end of the day, I would realize that my nightmare was reality. My grandmother used to tell me, "Just think of life as a tunnel. You're only going through." This had to have been the longest tunnel I'd ever traveled through. I couldn't even see the light shining at the end.

So there I was in the middle of this tunnel. It was cold and dark in there. I didn't have a friend to call on. Even if I did call on someone, it would just echo back to me. Funny thing about echoes is that if I asked a question, I never got an answer. The same question just kept echoing until it faded away.

Sometimes, things happen in our lives that are unexplainable. Every question doesn't necessarily have an answer. When God's working in your life, things become confusing. When you thought you knew or had it all, he'll sometimes set you back. Then you realize that you knew or had nothing at all. It's all a test, whether we understand it or not. That's how we know God's working.

8
DARNEST THINGS

Freedom. That was a word that was unfamiliar to me. A year later and my house is like a prison. Everything I did took place in that house. It had gotten so bad that I had developed a bad case of laziness. My house was nasty and I was confined to my own filth. It didn't bother Jeff because he was never there anyway.

Not only did I stop taking care of my house, I stopped taking care of myself as well. Yeah, I showered everyday, but that's the furthest I went. Why bother ironing if you're not going anywhere, right? Who was I getting prepped for anyway? Jeff, my own husband, wasn't looking at me. Sarah had to have been the cleanest, neatest thing in the house. Sometimes it seemed as if the worst I looked the better Jeff did.

"This place is a pig stein," my mother declared as she stepped over toys and piles of clothes.

"It's not that bad."

"It is. You've just been living in it for so long."

"Well it's not bothering anyone."

"It's bothering me."

"Well go home then, mom."

"Don't you sass me girl."

My mom, being the obsessively clean person that she is, started picking up around my house. Before I knew it, she was vacuuming and washing dishes. In less than two hours, my house was spotless and the washer and dryer were rolling.

"Mom, you didn't have to clean up."

"You didn't stop me either now did you?"

"No," I laughed.

"When's the last time you cooked? Cleaned yourself up?"

"For Who?"

"Jeff. Did you forget you had a husband?"

"Did he forget he had a wife?"

"Are you and Jeff having problems?"

"Yes, yes, yes! Jeff and I have been having major problems for over a year now. Major problems. You would not believe to what extent."

"Why didn't you say anything?"

"I've got enough drama in my life. I don't need yours and everyone else's."

"What's been going on?"

"Look, mom. I really don't want to talk about it."

"Well maybe if you fixed yourself up and cooked once in a while, he'd show some interest."

"And maybe if I was a cheap hooker on a street corner, he'd just buy my love for a little while."

"What does that mean?"

"It means that Jeff's a cheater, liar, womanizer, abuser, alcoholic, you name it. There. Are you happy?"

For the first time ever, my mother didn't have a come back. It was obvious that she didn't want to go toe-to-toe with a deranged woman. I had completely snapped. I didn't know who I was anymore. I couldn't tell if I was coming, going or even living for that matter. I had lost control of myself.

"I'm calling Dr. Renaldi. You need to see a doctor."

"I don't need a doctor, mother."

"Rita, you're sick."

"Yes. Yes. I am sick." I yelled. "Sick and tired of Jeff's abuse. I'm sick and tired of his infidelity. And I'm so tired of everyone depending on me. I'm only one person. I can't do everything. And what about me?"

"What about you, Rita? You're a free agent. Leave Jeff. Free yourself."

"It's not that easy, mom. You know that."

"Yes, I do know. When your dad put me through hell, I couldn't handle it. I knew that I had to call on friends and family for support. That was the time I needed them most."

"Well I'm not asking for help. No one can help me save my marriage."

"You think that you can do everything yourself, Rita. Family can't fix your problems, but they sure can help ease the pain. You know, make the transition a little smoother."

My mom was trying to make a point, but it wasn't helping. What in the hell was I transitioning into? I don't care how good my mom tried to make it sound it wasn't helping. The last thing I needed was my family blurting my business across Chicago. I could see the headlines now, "Husband, Jeff, Abuses Wife, Rita, while Autistic Daughter is in the House Which Happens to be Filthy." Leave it up to my mom and she's bound to include every detail, plus more.

"Mom, just let me deal with it my way."

"Under one condition."

"What's that?"

"You let me keep Sarah every other weekend while you go out."

"Go out where?"

"Anywhere. Two weekends out of the month are for you. Get out and do something. Get your hair and nails done. Go out to lunch with Shawntee. Just enjoy life for God's sake. Don't worry about Jeff. You just let him be. He'll come to his senses sooner or later."

"Can you and daddy handle Sarah by yourselves?"

"We handled you didn't we? You weren't autistic but you weren't sane either."

My mother may have been part right. It felt good having someone to talk to and spend time with. Jeff called and said that he would be working a private party, so that meant that he wasn't coming home that night. I asked my mom to stay the night with me. A mother's care was what I needed that night. She made my favorite dinner: meatloaf, mashed potatoes, and corn and buttermilk biscuits. We watched television and talked about old times.

After I put Sarah to bed, my mom and I nestled by the fireplace and toasted marshmallows. Now that Sarah was fast asleep, we talked about marriage and what the Bible says about it. I hadn't been to church in a while and maybe that was just what I needed: spiritual guidance. I've been pondering over what I should d in regards to my marriage, and here it was, already written.

"Pretty soon, Rita, God's going to bring you out of this war, undefeated. Don't let the devil steal your joy."

"I try not to, mom, but it's hard."

"You just have to stay prayerful. Put it in God's hands and let go."

"I'll give it a shot."

"Your faith only has to be the size of a mustard seed, Rita."

How big is a mustard seed? Because I don't know if I have that much faith. I've been out of the word for so long that I was afraid to ask God for anything. I wonder…if I ask for faith, and He gives it to me, would I be able to take it from there? Well it's worth a shot.

"God. Please give me faith the size of a mustard seed."

I think I've got it. Wait a minute. Can you ask God for faith? Ah hell, let me take my heathen ass back to church so I can learn the rules and regulations to this prayer thing.

Anyway. My mother and I had a fulfilling night. I learned things about her that I never knew. My mom never really got to know me as an adult, so everything was new to her. She never even knew the full details of how I met Jeff, until now.

Jeff snuck in the next morning and fixed breakfast for my mother, Sarah and I. You've got to commend him for trying. He put up a good front for my mother, not that she was buying it anyway.

"Breakfast was delicious, Jeff," my mom complimented.

"Thanks. I tried to put my foot in it."

"I hope not," I replied.

For all that I knew, Jeff could have meant that literately. He was trifling. Overall, the morning wasn't so bad after all. I give him an E for effort. He tried and failed. Not only was he a liar, he was a fake ass actor, too. Jeff always had to go over the top when trying to make himself look good.

I just wanted to ride his ass once my mother left, but it wasn't worth it. No matter what I said, Jeff would have thought he impressed my mother. I never had the guts to tell Jeff how my family truly felt about him. Besides, I didn't want to put them out there like that.

"So, Jeff. Are you working this weekend?"
"I work every weekend. Those are our busiest nights."
"So I guess I won't get to see you this weekend?"
"No," he answered, as if I ever got to see him on weekends.
"Oh okay. Was just wondering."
"Well now you know. I'm going to sleep. Please cut the ringer off if you leave out."

A real smart ass, he was. He knew that I wasn't going to leave the house. I never do. That's what Jeff liked most. He enjoyed having all of the fun while I drowned in my sorrows. Well not on this day. I sent Sarah with my mom and decided that it was time to take back my freedom.

While Jeff was asleep, I quietly packed my overnight bag. I left a note on the phone that read,

"Jeff. I'm going out for a couple of days to get a piece of mind. Sarah's at my mom's: if you care. Have a good time at work. Love you. Bye." He would find this note as soon as someone called the house.

That evening, I checked into a downtown suite where luxury was at my fingertips. I had a lot of money to play with, so I was determined to have some fun. I helped myself to a personal spa that included a facial, manicure, pedicure, and waxing and full body massage. It felt good to escape the prison I called home. I must admit that I hated to go back. I missed Sarah and felt guilty for sending her to my parent's. Sometimes I actually felt as if I didn't deserve a little piece of mind.

I was awed to see that Jeff was there when I returned home. I was certain that he would escape before my return. He didn't bother acknowledging Sarah and I as we walked in. It was as if we were ghosts. I didn't bother speaking either. Jeff was dead to me.

The atmosphere was cold for a few days and I couldn't figure out why. I don't know if Jeff was up to something, or if he was just salty because I went out without him. Who knows what was running through that empty brain of his.

"What's wrong with you? You've been kind of mute lately." I asked.

"Nothing's wrong with me. Did you ever think that maybe I just didn't feel like talking?"

"You mean to tell me that's possible?"

He didn't respond. He knew that I was being sarcastic and enjoying it. It was nice to actually get on his nerves for a change. Lord knows he's overworked mine.

I had decided to put Sarah in a special school and go back to work. I hadn't told Jeff, but my mom thought that it would be a good idea. She expressed her interests over a phone conversation one evening.

"That would be wise, Rita. She needs to interact with people other than us."

"You're right mom. Sarah's going to have this condition her whole life. She has to adapt to other environments. I can't keep her in the house forever."

"Keeping her in the house only says that you're ashamed of her."

"No, not at all. I could never be ashamed of her."

"Well send her to school then."

My mother was right as usual. It was as if I was hiding Sarah from the world. Sarah wasn't going to be a little girl forever, and it was up to me to teach her the ways of the world. Although this would be a difficult task, it was still my duty as her mother.

There were a couple of schools near the downtown area that were convenient for me. It's funny how I passed these places daily and never noticed them. I was amazed at how many children had the same problem that Sarah had. Some cases were even worse. The teachers were very diligent in helping me understand their curriculum and methods of teaching.

I was a little skeptical about leaving Sarah behind. It was like her first day of school, all over again. She had a short hissy fit before I left, but the instructors assured me that they were skilled in dealing with cases like Sarah's.

"I'll see you when I get off of work. Okay Sarah?"

"See you mommy. Okay. I'll see you mommy. See you."

It tore me up to leave her for a minute. I sat in the car, contemplating if I should go back in or not. Finally, I started my engine, and headed for work.

"Surprise," everyone yelled as I walked through the door. How did they know that I was coming back? There were balloons, food, and a huge cake that read, World's Greatest Boss. Welcome Back." It felt good to be back. I had truly missed Candy Records.

I was showered with cards and flower all that week. Everyone's heart poured out to me as I tackled a disturbing life. Every notion was greatly appreciated. I couldn't have asked for a better staff.

When I broke the news to Jeff, he reacted just as I expected. He was upset at the fact that I had returned to work. Although I explained it to him, he skipped over the whole Sarah going to school part.

"You should be happy that I'm going back to work, Jeff. At least you won't have to look in my face all day."

"So that's what this is about? You call yourself running away from me?"

"No. I call myself retuning back to my career. Something you don't know anything about."

"I have a career."

"No. You have a job, and barely that. One day you'll realize that tips ain't enough to pay the bills around here."

Jeff's palm slapped clean across my face. I could taste the blood from my busted lip. I lowered my head and proceeded to the bathroom to clean myself up. Why didn't I react? Why was I so afraid of him? Maybe in the back of my mind, I knew that this day was coming.

There was no way that I could hide my fat, pink lip at work the next day. I was embarrassed by the stares and whispers. How could I be so powerful at work, and yet so hopeless at home? I had lost control and there was no way around it.

There was something in the back of my mind that led me to believe that Jeff's father was abusive towards his mother. This isn't something he just picked up overnight. I had questions and I needed answers; now. One evening while Jeff was working late, I did the unthinkable. I called his mother. Jeff never gave me her number directly, but the number that appeared on my phone bill was allegedly hers.

"Hello?" a voice answered on the other end. The woman sounded young: around thirty-one thirty-two.

"Hi. I'm trying to reach Mrs. Ruth Bridges. Do I have the right number?"

"No, but I'm her daughter-in-law. How may I help you?"

"My name is Rita. Rita Bridges. I'm calling in regards to your brother-in-law, Jeff Bridges."

The woman laughed as if I had told a joke. It didn't dawn on me that Jeff said he only had a sister. If this was true, how could she be his sister-in-law?

"Jeff is not my brother-in-law. He's my husband. Now seriously, who is this? Is this some kind of joke?"

"Oh this is no joke. Jeff is my husband. We've been married for six years now," I protested.

"We couldn't possibly be talking about the same man. Jeff and I have been married for thirteen years. We were high school sweethearts. We married immediately after graduation."

I paused for a moment to recollect my thoughts. I didn't recall Jeff mentioning a high school sweetheart. This had to have been some sort of joke. For a second, I was under the assumption that Jeff had a sister that was just messing with my head. So I decided to play along with it.

"Just to be certain we're not talking about the same Jeff, what's your husband's full name?" I asked.

"Jeffrey Michael Bridges Jr.," the woman replied.

She was right on the money. That was my husband's whole name. I was in disbelief. Word's could not explain what was going through my head. My heart sank and I could feel the lump growing in my throat.

"Hello?" she asked.

"Yes. I'm here. I truly don't know how to say this, but I think that we may be married to the same man."

"That's absurd. Who are you and what kind of stunt are you trying to pull?"

"My name is Rita Bridges and I live in Chicago. I met Jeff almost seven years ago in New Orleans. We have a six year old daughter."

"Does his mother know anything about this?"

"As far as I know. I've never met anyone in his family."

"Can you describe him?"

"Of course."

I went on to tell her all about Jeff. I told her how I met him and where he worked back in New Orleans. We compared birth dates, birthmarks, scars, tattoos and even the way he wrote his signature. It was the same Jeff all right.

My world came crumbling down. Life as I knew it was over. How could this be? This woman, Tina Bridges, was married to my husband. She even had two boys with him. Actually, I had married her husband.

"That son-of-a-bitch. How could he? What was he thinking?" Tina cried.

"Where have you been for the last six years?" I asked.

"Right here. I was right here all along."

Apparently, Jeff was in Chicago starting his own business. He told her that he had opened a new nightclub and had to stay in Chicago for a year to monitor the business.

"He called me everyday and sent money to pay the bills. Jeff is so damn slick, that I never questioned what he was doing. I was always afraid of knowing the truth."

"And the other years?" I insisted.

"We were separated for two years. When we got back together, that's when he announced his plans to go to Chicago. I've been there several times to see him."

"Where did you stay?"

"At his house."

"You mean my house?"

"I guess."

I was furious. How could I be so stupid? She wasn't at a lost because she was a stay-at-home mom. Jeff had always taken care of her and his two boys. I was humiliated. This woman knew more about Jeff than I did. She knew his past. She knew his family. I was non-existent.

"So what now I asked?"

"Is Jeff there with you now?"

"No. He's never home."

"I don't know what you're going to do, but I'm not doing anything. Jeff owns this house, two buildings, and a motel. I was married to him first. Get your own husband."

She had a point. If she married him thirteen years ago and never divorced him, our marriage wasn't legal and binding. So the question was, "What do I do?" I wasn't prepared to argue with Jeff or listen to him lie his way out of it. Out of all of the pain that Jeff put me through, you would think that I was happy to lose him. I wasn't. I had been bamboozled and I was determined to get revenge.

Tina and I talked all day and I learned more and more about Jeff. I was shocked to learn that Jeff's wife was fighting ovarian cancer and that Jeff's wife was fighting ovarian cancer and that Jeff's wife were still abusive towards her.

"I always knew that he was up to something I just didn't care. I didn't have the education or training to get a good job, so Jeff always took care of me."

"Do you still love him?" I asked.

"I don't know. I used to. I was crazy about Jeff when I met him. Now, I think I'm just plain crazy."

"I know what you mean, Tina. He does me the same way. It's time for me to cut him loose."

"What are you going to do?"

"I don't know, but he might be home real soon."

"Be careful."

She was more afraid of Jeff than I was. I could hear her trembling on the other end. Her fears only heightened the situation. It was almost as if she knew the outcome.

Jeff came in and I tried to act normal. I gathered my thoughts while fixing dinner. As much as I tried to keep my composure, I couldn't.

"Jeff. We need to talk."

"Talk later. I'm tired."

"No. We need to talk now."

"What woman?"

"Whose Louisiana call is this on my phone bill?"

"It's my mother's number. I tell you this every month."

"Well I called your mother today."

"You did what?" he asked in outrage.

"I called your mother."

"And what did she say?" he asked taking two steps towards me.

I was scared. I knew that he was about to put his hands on me. Sarah was in her room playing and I didn't think to just leave.

"I talked to your other wife. Yeah. She told me everything. I know about your house and buildings and motels and your sons."

"You bitch. You have no right."

He reached out for me but I jumped behind the table just in time.

"I have every right, you low-down, dirty bastard. I'm taking your ass to court. I'm having you put in jail. It's over for you, buddy."

Jeff stormed out the kitchen, and like a jackass, I followed behind him.

"Don't walk away, now. What do you have to say for yourself?"

I gasped as I saw the lamp come flying across the room. It happened so fast that it didn't even look like he had done it. The rest was a blur.

So here I am. I can hear all of the machines and monitors beeping around me. Sarah's voice echoed in my ears. My mother's cries rang through my head. Even worse, I didn't know exactly how much damage Jeff had caused. I didn't feel a thing. Could breathe, but I couldn't move. You could hear the doctor's call, "She's non-responsive." Then there was silence. Everything stopped; the doctor's, Sarah, my mother, and the monitors. I had faded away from all that had life.

9
RUDE AWAKENING

After forty-two days of nothing, I woke up. Unfortunately, no one was there. My eyes focused as my ears searched the room for familiar sounds. Nothing. It seemed like it was just yesterday when Sarah called my name from afar.

I laid there for hours before the nurses realized I was awake. I was afraid to move or even try to speak. The day and hour was unknown. Life had been non-existent for over a month, which actually felt like a day.

Time had lapsed and the world had gone on without me. The doctor's contacted my mother, who wasn't home at the time. I could clearly hear and see everyone moving around me. The doctor ordered tests to monitor my progress.

"Mrs. Bridges. Can you hear me?" he asked.

I wanted to respond, but I didn't know how. It was like starting over as a baby. I couldn't even move my lips to form a word. My muscles were weak and I couldn't even force myself to talk.

"Mrs. Bridges," he continued. "If you can hear me, blink once."

I closed my eyes and slowly opened them back up. That was a big step seeing as though I was able to communicate with the doctor. I could feel him touching my feet, legs, arms and hands.

"Mrs. Bridges. Your mother's on the way to see you. Do you think that you can say something? If so, blink."

I didn't blink. It wasn't that I couldn't talk, I was just afraid to try. Besides, all of the tubes that were in my mouth made it harder to try.

I froze at the sound of little feet running up the hall. My heart pounded as I waited to hear Sarah's voice but there was nothing. Then finally, I heard the voice of a toddler talking with a gentleman in the hall. It wasn't my Sarah.

Then my eyes focused at the silhouette in the door. It was my mother. She the biggest smile and her eyes were filled with tears.

"Thank you Jesus," she cried out.

A little girl stepped from behind her, holding a teddy bear. It was my Sarah. I could feel the tears rolling down my face. She climbed onto the bed and kissed me on the check.

"You were sleep a long time. Long time, mommy. Long time."

"Praise God, she's awake now," my mom said.

The physician called my mom in the hall, so that he could discuss what was going on. I admired Sarah's courage as she in there with me. She was so beautiful. It seemed as if she had fattened up a little, too. I wanted her as she rocked and sang to the teddy bear.

I wanted to try and speak but now was not the time. I didn't want to scare Sarah if anything went wrong. I knew that I had to take baby steps to a full successful recovery.

My mother was extremely supportive over the next few weeks. According to the doctor's, the coma and trauma, to the head, caused some brain damage. They weren't sure if I would redevelop all of my skills. I was mobile and able to walk with a walker. My nerves were shot, so I did a lot of trembling. I still wasn't able to talk though.

Sometimes I found myself mumbling like a baby. Talking as going to take an extra effort. Even when I tried to speak, I would shake so badly that I would start to drool. This was where I became embarrassed. I was already ashamed that I would even put myself in this position. My mother had to take care of my daughter and me. I was determined to get back to normal and raise my own daughter.

My mother informed me that Sarah was no longer in school. I had moved my parents so far away that they couldn't make the commute everyday. I was hurt that I had to put my mother through so much. If I had only left Jeff in New Orleans, none of this would have happened.

"Rita, baby. I'm getting ready to go home. You did god today. I love you." My mom kissed me on my head and went about her way.

I laid there, in that cold, empty room, thinking of how things could have been different. I wondered what had happened to Jeff. I was certain that he had fled back to New Orleans. I thought about the family that he already had established. I knew in my heart that he had gone back to them. I was okay with that. I never wanted to be with him again. What I wanted was revenge. There was no way that I was going to let him walk so easily. Not after what he had done to me.

As my therapy went on, my progress increased. I was able to talk, very slowly, but I was talking. Most importantly, my mom and Sarah understood me.

"I'm proud of you, Rita. You're doing good."

"Thanks," I replied.

"You have to get well so that you can get back to work. You know how much you love that job."

"Not as much as I love you and Sarah," I finally said.

"I know dear."

"Jeff?"

"What about him?"

"Jeff!" I repeated.

"I know. We'll take care of him when you get well."

My mother already knew where I was coming from. She knew that I wanted Jeff's head on a platter. I could tell that her wishes were the same. My father, on the other hand, had taken things to a whole new level. He hired a private investigator. We all were determined to get answers and reveal the truth.

After six months of therapy, I was ready to return home. My parents picked me up from the hospital and insisted that I stayed with them for a while. I wanted to go home. I hadn't seen my house in seven months. My mother checked on it regularly and assured me that everything was still in tact. She said that she had even cleaned up from that devastating night.

I agreed to go home with my parents for two weeks. I wanted to ease their minds and reassure them that I was capable of taking care of Sarah and myself. I was just happy to be out of the hospital and away from the doctors. Regular doctor visits had been scheduled to monitor my performance.

"It's time to take care of business, Rita," my dad said.

"What do you mean daddy?"

You know what I mean. It's time to take care of Mr. Jeff Bridges."

My dad was about business. He wanted me to sue Jeff for everything that he had. I explained to my parents that Jeff was married before me and that it was possible that I was entitled to nothing.

"This is crazy. There's got to be something we could do," my mom protested.

"There is. We sit and wait. The investigator ill find out all we need to know. In the meantime, Rita, you need to get in contact with the other wife."

Okay. I used to think that my dad was crazy, but now I know he is. He explained how there was a way to get rid of Jeff, and keep al of his money. Tina wanted Jeff out of her life too, but she needed the money. I didn't need any support from Jeff. I just wanted him locked up.

IT was days before I contacted Tina. I had a friend call from his phone. My friend's number wasn't listed in case Jeff answered instead of Tina. My friend disguised his voice and asked for Mrs. Tina Bridges. He was turned down quickly, but we were able to verify Jeff's location.

The private investigator prepared to gather facts for court. His trip to New Orleans was brief. Upon his return, we learned that Jeff was living happily ever after with Tina. Convincing her to go against Jeff in court was out of the question.

"What do I do now, Shawntee?"

"I say, make a trip to New Orleans."

"Are you crazy, or do you just want men dead?"

"Don't go alone, stupid. Take the private investigator and a friend or family member. Stake outside of his house until he leaves. Once he leaves, knock on the door and introduce yourself. Tina will let you in and then you can go from there."

"That's too risky. I could get her and myself killed in the process."

"Well you've got to do something."

"I'll consult with the private investigator and see what he suggests."

Honestly, I wasn't well enough to pursue a lawsuit. It was possible that all of the drama could have caused a relapse. I decided to let Jeff be, for the time being. I was more concerned about my health and the well being of my child.

Sarah never had any negative reactions to what went on. I'm not certain if she was aware of the things that went on around her. To be on the safe side, I took her to see a child psychiatrist that specialized in autistic children. She had some very interesting things to say.

"Whether you believe it or not, Mrs. Bridges, Sarah knows everything that goes on around her," she told me.

"She never shows emotion or ask any questions, though."

"Just because she's aware, doesn't necessarily means that she understands."

"So will all of the trauma have a negative affect on her?"

"She can't always differentiate what's negative and positive. Everything is practically the same with Rita. Especially since she sees it almost everyday. It is what it is."

"In that case, how would she ever know if anyone's trying to hurt her or not?"

"She's like a newborn baby. Just like the doctors had to teach you to walk and talk again, you have to teach her to feel."

"That doesn't make any sense."

"Mrs. Bridges, may I call you Rita?"

"Yes."

"Rita. Babies pick up emotions by watching us. They learn to associate smiles with happiness, frowns with sadness, and kisses with love."

"So I have to teach her these things all over again?"

"Think back to when Sarah was a baby. It's supposed to come natural. You do hug and kiss Sarah don't you?"

I stopped and thought for a moment. Then I fell back in my chair in shame. The truth was, I was not as nurturing as I should be. I had neglected Sarah's feelings by being consumed with my own drama. Truth be told, I was just as bad a parent as Jeff.

"No. Not really," I responded.

"Well why not?"

"I don't know. I guess I've been too wrapped up in myself. How could I be so selfish?"

"This doesn't necessarily make you a bad parent. You still take care of Sarah on a daily basis."

"Yeah, but that's because I have to. Not necessarily because I want to. I'm a bad mother."

The reality of it all put me in a state of shock. I burst out in tears at the thought of it. Sarah got up and walked over to the fish tank nearby. I watched her as she identified each type of fish in the tank.

"She's very intelligent," the doctor said.

"Yes, she is."

"You should go over there and give her a big hug and kiss. It's not too late to be a good mom."

I sat there for a moment because I was afraid of how Sarah would react. Slowly, I walked over to her, kneeled down, and gave her a big hug. In return, she kissed my cheek. It was just that simple.

So there I was taking my first steps into a new life. I wanted to be a good mother to Sarah. I yearned to give her the foundation she needed to be a good mother and wife, if ever possible.

"Do children with her condition ever grow up to get married and have children on their own?"

"It depends on how extreme the case is. Most likely, no. Most autistic adults stay at home with their parents. Often times, they're still in a childlike phase."

"I'm sure that most parents of autistic children are overbearing and very protective of their adult children."

"Yes. They're still your babies."

I had a lot of learning to do. If I was going to be a good mother to Sarah, I had to be as knowledgeable as possible about her condition. This was the only way I'd be able to provide adequate support for Sarah.

The doctor suggested that I get Sarah back in school immediately. This was to assure that she wouldn't lose her social skills. I agreed to take some classes as well to learn new ways of learning with Sarah.

Returning o work was strange for me. My co-workers weren't so happy to see me. Everyone was capable of carrying out the business without me. Some felt that I didn't deserve the position. I can't help but think that they were right. I've had so many personal issues affect my attendance and performance on the job.

My parents and Shawntee were very supportive during my time of need. My work was backed up and I had to pull doubles before Rick found out and had a fit. No one at the company was willing to help me play catch up. Instead, everyone watched and whispered. I knew that they were waiting for me to fall flat on my face.

I was determined to prove them wrong. Not only that, I had to prove to myself that I was still capable of getting the job done. It was hard trying to play catch up at work and with Sarah at the same time. I refused to neglect my job and Sarah again.

After a few months, I ran back into a brick wall. My father grew ill and my mother had to tend to him. I knew that she wasn't going to be able to keep Sarah anymore. I had to step up and help my mom take care of daddy.

"Don't worry about your father, Rita. You just concentrate on work and Sarah," she said.

"I can do that and help you with daddy, too."

I volunteered my weekends off to stay at my parent's house. I did the cooking and cleaning while my mother stayed by daddy's bedside. We didn't know what was wrong and my dad refused to go to the hospital.

"Mom. Dad can't lie in that bed forever. We have to get him to a doctor."

"No. It ain't nothing a little Echinacea and green tea can't help."

"Mom, you have to let go of those southern treatments. This is no common cold."

"There is no ailment that a little aloe vera juice can't heal."

"I'm calling the hospital."

I went against my parents' wishes and contacted the physician. After telling them his symptoms, they instructed me to get my father to the hospital immediately. I dressed my father and called for an ambulance. I was too nervous to drive him. My mother rode with him, and Sarah and I took a cab.

Upon arrival, my father had been admitted into the intensive care unit. Monitors were hooked up to my father. My mother went into an immediate panic. I couldn't keep my own composure, let alone calm my mom down. The doctor's and nurses zoomed pass us without saying a word.

After sitting in the waiting room for hours, the doctor returned with a solemn look upon his face. I knew instantly that it was bad news.

"Your husband and father has pneumonia," he said.

"So how long will he be sick?"

"We don't know. You see, it turns out that he also has lung cancer."

"But he doesn't smoke," my mom replied.

"Yeah, but he did used to own a tavern in his twenties."

"How many years did he work there?" the doctor asked.

"About eighteen," my mom replied.

"Well that explains it. Second hand smoke is just as dangerous. His case is severe. When's the last time he's seen a physician?"

My mom didn't answer. She never liked going to the doctor and my father was the same way. I knew that she was ashamed to tell the truth.

"Mom?" I asked.

"Early nineties. But he's been healthy ever since."

"He's always had a really bad cough, doctor. He blamed it on the smog," I volunteered.

"His immune system is very weak, and if he doesn't get well soon, the combination of the two could kill him."

"Oh my God. The devil is a liar," my mother screamed.

"Yes, he is mom." I pulled her close to calm her down. "So what do we do now doctor?"

"We wait it out. Our staff is doing everything possible to get your father back to a good bill of health."

"Thank you. Come on mom. Let's go home."

"No. I'm not leaving my husband," she screamed.

"She can stay the night with him."

I left my mom at the hospital and caught a cab back to their house. After feeding Sarah, I cleaned the kitchen and went into my parents' room to snoop around. I don't know why I felt an urge to be nosy, but my mom's reaction told me that she knew more than she claimed to have known.

After two hours of searching, I found nothing but old pictures and letters from my dad when he was in the service. Finally, I came across a black brief case in the back of the closet. Inside of it were important documents. Mostly insurance papers and receipts. I opened another compartment inside of the suitcase and there were three prescriptions for medications dated back to nineteen-ninety. There were also doctor's statements diagnosing my father with lung cancer. My mother had known all along.

I could see how my dad disregarded his illness. He was stubborn that way. He used to always say,

"My momma and daddy never saw no doctor and they were just fine." Then he'd go on to tell me how people just died of old age. As if that was ever an illness.

The very next day, I took Sarah to school before going to the hospital. She had seen enough in her time; I certainly didn't want her to have to see more. I called Shawntee on my way to the hospital to let her know what was going on.

"Hey Shawntee, it's Rita."

"I know. I have caller id. What's up?"

"My dad's in the hospital."

"Why? Your mom said that he just had a cold."

Well it turns out that he has pneumonia."

"Pneumonia?"

"Yeah, and lung cancer."

"At the same time?"

"After going through my parent's things, I discovered that he was diagnosed back in nineteen-ninety."

"And let me guess. Your mom didn't tell you."

"Of course not."

"Well you know how your parents are."

"Yeah. Stubborn."

"So how is he?"

"He should be okay. I'm on my way to go see him now. My mom stayed at the hospital with him last night."

"Well call me back when you leave."

"Okay. I'm going to try to make it in to work by lunchtime. I'll call you."

"Okay. Bye."

"Bye."

I walked up to the front desk and requested a pass for the intensive care unit. They told me that he had been moved and redirected me to another floor. When I got to the third floor, there was nothing but offices. I didn't recognize anyone so I got on the elevator and headed up to ICU anyway.

My dad's bed was empty and I didn't see my mom anywhere. I stopped a nurse to find out where they were. I stopped a nurse to find out where they were. Again I was redirected to the third floor. This time, she told me to go to suite three thirteen. There, I found the doctor that was treating my father.

"Mrs. Bridges. Please. Have a seat. I was just trying to contact you at home."

"Oh, I'm sorry. I stayed at my parents' home last night. Look, I found some information that might help with your treatment. It turns out that my father was diagnosed with cancer back in nineteen-ninety. I was thinking that maybe you could contact that hospital and request those records."

"Mrs. Bridges. I'm sorry to inform you, but your father passed this morning."

"What?" I screamed.

"He was just too weak. The virus took over his body and, well...?"

"So that's it? My father is dead? Just like that?"

"Yes. I'm sorry."

"Where is he now?"

"He's downstairs at the morgue."

"Where's my mother?"

"She's in the chapel having prayer."

"Can I see him?"

The doctor escorted me to the basement where the morgue was located. I felt weak in the knees as we walked down the long ark hall. Then pulled back the sheets so that I could view my father's remains. I fell to my knees and screamed,

"Oh God. Why him?"

"Why not him?" a voice replied form behind.

It was my mo6ther. She walked over to me and pulled me up from the floor. She took another look at my father and kissed him on the head.

"Why not him, Rita? His work is done here on Earth. Now he can walk around heaven all day. Who are we to question the work of God?"

We stood there and held each other for a while. Finally, the doctor suggested that we go back to his office and prepare to make arrangements. Upstairs in his office, we called a funeral home to pick up the remains. Remains. Hmmm. It was daddy just yesterday. Everything started going so fast. I didn't have time to mourn.

My mother and I spent that evening calling family, friends and church members. Who knew that the next few days would be harder to deal with than death itself? People stopped by to offer condolences and bring food. My mother wasn't in a friendly mood and insisted that I took care of all the arrangements.

I didn't know anything about funeral arrangements. The last death that we had had was my sister's, and I was too young to take part in the arrangements. I had to pick a suit, casket, flowers, church, everything. I knew to have the funeral at my parents' church. The only problem was that the church was too small to hold all of the people that were expected to attend. So I decided to have previewing the day before at the funeral home.

I never knew that I had to go to the cemetery and make separate arrangements for the plot. I always thought that the funeral home did everything. After looking at caskets, flowers and gravesites, I was torn. Everything started to look the same. A box was a box. A whole was a whole. A carnation was a carnation.

My parents had small policies and I was confined to a tight budget. Who knew that burying someone could cost so much? I wasn't hung up on prices. I just wanted to lay my daddy to rest.

On the day of the funeral, I was mentally exhausted. People had been in and out of my parents' house all week. Had made so many trips to the florists, printers and cemetery that my car was giving out on me.

The limousines picked us up around one o'clock. It was pouring down raining. When we walked into the church, it was packed wall to wall. There were aunts, uncles, and cousins from all over. We made it down the aisle to the casket where my mom paused. She touched daddy's hand and kissed his head.

"Good night sweet prince. 'Till we meet again."

She took it better than I thought she would. I took a quick glance at him and sat down. I was doing pretty well. Sarah turned to me and had a strange look on her face.

"What is it, Sarah?"

"I want to see. Granddaddy. I want to see."

She did get a chance to see him because we zoomed by so fast. I actually didn't want her to see him. I granted her those wishes and we went back up before they closed the casket. She stood there. Just staring at him. Then she asked,

"Can I kiss him? Mommy. Granddaddy. Kiss him?"

I picked her up and hovered her over the casket. She kissed his cheek and I saw a tear drop down her face. Sarah was crying. That was the first time Sarah had shown emotion without anyone initiating it. It was then that I knew. There were people that had a direct effect on Sarah. My father was the only man that Sarah had ever connected with.

The burial followed the service. You could see the processional in the side mirror for miles and miles back. My mom was stable and she kept Sarah nearby. They read a scripture, said a prayer, and lowered my dad into the ground.

"Ashes to ashes. Dust to dust." the preacher called.

At that moment it hit me. This was it. My dad was gone. One day he was alive, and the next day he was dead. And now, it was time for me to say goodbye, forever. I started to tremble and I could feel someone grab me. I threw back my head, opened my mouth, and screamed. Every pain that I felt came out in that scream. I cried out to the clouds. And at that very second, everything around me stopped.

10
MAKEOVER MADNESS

I never knew that death could be so hard to cope with. It's been almost a year since my father's death. My mother, on the other hand, was a lot stronger than I was. She had seen many people come and go, including her parents, daughter and now her husband. She accepted death long ago. Now me? Death was my worst enemy. It had taken my sister and now my father. And for that, I was so damn bitter.

At this point in my life, there was nothing or no one that could do a damn thing for me. I was a thirty-three year old, angry black woman with a grudge. Mad at the world and willing to take anybody down with me. Life had dealt me a badass hand, and no matter how skilled I was, I ended up reneging.

'So now what?' I asked myself. I went on to my daily routine of work and home. Sarah was a healthy eight-year-old and for that, I was grateful. Things could always be worse than what they are. I still had a job, food in the refrigerator, a roof over my head, and my health.

Shawntee was either concerned about my well being or shooting for world's best friend because she stopped by everyday. She was single again so visiting Sarah and I was the highlight of her day.

"Rita. You can't sit around moping forever. Get out. Do something."

"Something like what?"

"I don't know. You need a man."

"No I don't. I'm still married, remember?"

"Legally, you're not. And stop sounding so damn dry."

"I am dry. Dry and bitter."

"About what?"

"Everything, Shawntee. I don't know. I'm just so damn angry."

"Is this about your father's death?"

"No. Yes. No. It's more than that."

"Well what is it, Rita?"

"I don't know."

"You do know. And whatever it is, you're ashamed to admit it. That's why you're so damn mad."

"You just think you know everything, don't you?"

"I do. But it's not about me, it's about you."

"I miss Jeff."

"What?" Shawntee shrieked.

"I miss Jeff. I know it sounds crazy, but I do."

"Rita. Listen to yourself. This man almost killed you. You were in a coma for God's sake."

"Calm down, Shawn. I didn't say that I was going to get him back. I'm just admitting that I miss him. I don't like being alone."

"You were alone when he was here."

"I know, but…I don't know. It's a bad feeling turning over to cold sheets."

"Don't you think I know that, Rita? I've been alone for months now. Maybe you just need to be by yourself right now."

"You may be right."

"If you become desperate for attention, you become vulnerable and start accepting anything."

Shawntee definitely had a point there. Sometimes it's best to be alone. Jumping from one man to another won't solve our problems; it just creates more. Why do we do it? Because most of us have had drama in our lives for so long that once it's gone, we search for something or someone else to fill that void. Once it's filled, we realize that it was the same all along. Drama.

This is how we come to the conclusions that all men are dogs. Truth is, some of us are just shopping for the wrong pets. Too often, we find a man that's almost exactly like the one before him. So where do we go wrong? We immediately run back to the same pet shop and buy another dog. Instead, we should wait before making an exchange. Research the pets a little more and take the time to establish which pet best suits our needs. After setting your standards, you're ready to shop. Hell, this time you might come back with a rabbit or bird instead. Just stay away from the snakes. They can be tricky.

Myself. I was at an in between stage. It was time to decide if I wanted a dog or a fish. Just when I thought I knew everything about men, I find out I've got the game all twisted. I had been cursed, beaten and drug through the dirt. You would think that I had had enough, but I hadn't. Something inside still made me love my husband. My mind told me 'no', but my heart said 'yes'.

I knew that I would have to face Jeff again one day. I had informed the investigator of my father's death and asked him to hold off on the investigation. He had started back calling and inquiring about the job.

"Mrs. Bridges, you can't put this of too much longer," he said.

"I know. I just don't have the time right now."

"Well we handle the bulk of the work, so there's really not much for you to do except consult an attorney."

"I'll tell you what. Call me back in to days and we'll be able to work something out."

"Okay, Mrs. Bridges. I'll do that."

My past kept coming back to haunt me and I knew that I had to close that chapter of my life for good. I was just so afraid of knowing the truth. I had a gut feeling that there was so much more to this story. This was about to be a big ugly mess that I didn't want to see.

My work at the record company was becoming more challenging and I was afraid that I wasn't going to be able to hang. There were about four people on the job waiting for me to fail so that they could take my position. Rick made a surprise visit to the office one day and I was not on the ball.

"How's everything, Rita?" he asked.

"Everything's peachy, Rick."

"Not from what I hear."

"You're still getting paid aren't you?"

"That doesn't mean my clients are happy. I've been getting a lot of calls to New York, Rita, and I must say, I'm not pleased with you performance at all."

"Well, you know my father died and I've been dealing with a lot of personal issues."

"Rita. When I put you in that position you were young, vibrant, and driven. What happened? You've fallen off!"

"I'm just dealing with so much, Rick. You know that."

"Look. I put all of my trust in you when I put you in that chair. Maximize your success by minimizing your excuses."

"You're right, Rick. I won't let you down."

"Don't. I'd hate to have to fire you. You know, with your personal issues and all." He laughed in a notion to mock me and tapped me on the head with a stack of papers. "Stop watching those soap operas, kiddo. You're getting to dramatic."

"Will do, sir."

I was embarrassed that my boss had to fly all the way from the east coast just to put me in my place. When I stepped out of the office, all eyes were on me. All of a sudden, I didn't feel so in control. It was true. I had lost my drive. Hell, I had lost my will to live.

"Mom, I don't know what's wrong with me," I said to my mom that evening.

"Come here, Rita."

I climbed onto my mom's sofa and laid my head on her lap. Sarah was in her bedroom playing with the doll that my father had bought. My mother brushed my hair and sang a hymn for a while.

"Do you remember when you were a little girl, and your father bought us those matching pink dresses?"

"Yeah mom. You hated those dresses."

"I loved yours. I just hated mine."

"Why? They were cute."

"They were pink," she laughed.

"What's wrong with pink?"

"When you think of pink, you think of babies and little girls. Pink is so soft, sweet, and innocent. But as you grow from a little girl to a woman, things change. You start to try different combinations of pink: pink and purple, pink and white, pink and yellow. Then one day you grow up, and what you perceive as pink is no longer pink. When you become a woman, a real woman, you become bolder, stronger. That's what happens to your pinks. They become bolder and stronger and the next thing you know, you're wearing rose or fuchsia."

"So what you're saying is be bolder, stronger. Learn to stand on my own two feet. I get it."

"What I'm saying to you Rita is, real women don't wear pink. Are you a woman? A real woman?"

That was a lot to swallow. We get older and assume that we're automatically men or women. Real womanhood doesn't come with age. It takes trials and tribulations in your life to help you establish where you truly stand. I had overcome so many things over the past few years that had prepared me for this moment. So on that day, I declared myself a woman. A real woman.

I went home that night with a new attitude. No longer was I the devil's doormat. I was confident, fierce, and a little cocky. I pitied the fool that challenged my womanhood. So what next? I called the private investigator.

"So you're sure that you're ready for me to follow through with the case," he asked.

"Absolutely. Be sure to notify me immediately upon your arrival."

"Will do Mrs. Bridges."

"Talk to you in a few days."

"Until then."

Shawntee and I went on a shopping spree the following weekend. She had just got her income tax check and it was burning her pockets. I bought Sarah a spring jacket and some shoes for school. I was more so shopping for a new wardrobe to match my new attitude.

"Not much is going to change in your style, Rita. You already wear some pretty fancy stuff."

"I was thinking of trying some bolder colors. I want to get out of the usual browns, blacks, blues and grays."

"You should wear more skirts this spring and summer. Show off those legs."

"I've been reading a lot of fashion magazines lately. Vibrant colors are in. I've been seeing a lot of reds and turquoise in the stores."

"I hear blacks and whites are making a comeback."

"Not in my closet," I laughed.

"Clothes aren't your problem, Rita. You need to learn how to accessorize."

"What do you suggest?"

"Well. Your chain and locket is cute but it doesn't go with everything."

"It's gold. How can it not go with everything?"

"Lose the gold. If you've noticed, costume jewelry doesn't look so bad. It makes the outfit."

"I don't really know how to shop for that type of stuff."

"Just match the colors in the jewelry to your clothes. It's just that simple. Throw in a pair of shoes and a funky, little handbag and you're in the mix."

"In the mix? You're so outdated."

"This from a woman who's had the same exact haircut since high school."

"What's wrong with my hair?" I asked.

"Nothing. It's just that you never switch up. You wear the same cut everyday, down to the last curl."

"I like my haircut."

"Don't get me wrong. It's pretty. Just go out on a limb and try something new."

I thought about it for a minute. If I was going to be bold, I had to be open for change as well. There was a beauty shop inside of the mall, so I decided to pay them a visit while Shawntee took Sarah to the food court for lunch.

"So, Rita, what would you like done?" asked the beautician.

"Anything. Just make it pretty."

"Anything?"

"Feel free to be creative. Classy, but creative."

"So a weave is out of the question?"

"Indefinitely."

I sat in that chair and watched her perm, cut and color my hair. She said that I was going to have auburn highlights, with a metallic-like shimmer. I was afraid that I would look like a clown afterwards. Once the cut was complete, I moved into the chair of the make-up artist.

When it came to make-up I was pretty plain. A little lip-gloss and liner was all that I required.

The make-up artist spun my chair around so that I could get a good look at myself. I couldn't believe my eyes. I looked like an entirely different person. I felt like a supermodel. Shawntee and Sarah were standing in the hall waiting to see the final product. Heads turned as I exited the salon. Sarah gasped and ran towards me with he arms opened wide.

"Oooh. Pretty."

"I look pretty Sarah?"

"Yes. Pretty like on TV. Like on TV."

"How do I look?" I asked Shawntee.

For a moment, I thought something was wrong. Shawntee just stood there with her hands over her mouth. I could see the tears gathering in her eyes.

"What's wrong? I don't look good?"

"You look amazing," she finally answered.

"Amazing?"

"Simply amazing."

"So I'm hot, huh?"

"Don't ruin the moment by ego-tripping."

Men gawked at my beauty as I strolled through the mall. I had a new look to go with my new attitude. This was the new me. The real woman. I had arrived and it felt damn good to be here.

I stopped at the cookie shop to purchase Sarah some cookies on the way home. A gentleman approached me as I was leaving the store.

"Excuse me, miss. Don't I know you from somewhere?"

I scanned up and down his robust frame and shrugged my shoulders. He was my height, which was kind of short for a guy. He was cute in the face, but I didn't recognize him at all.

"No. I don't think we've met before."

"Don't you have an aunt named Ola Mae?"

"Yes. My mother's sister."

"Sister Ola Mae is a member of my church, New Mountain of Hope M.B.C."

"Yes. Yes. I've been there before."

"Derrick Jackson. I play the bass guitar for the choir." He stretched out his hand and initiated a shake.

"Oh. Nice to meet you."

"Pleasure's all mine."

"Well, I have to go. It's starting to rain outside."

"Okay. You have yourself a good evening."

"Likewise." I reached for the doorknob and he began to speak again.

"We're having our family and friends day this upcoming Sunday. I would like to extend an invitation for you to come. I'm sure your aunt would be glad to see you there. I know I would."

"Thanks. I'll see if I can make it. Nice meeting you. Again."

"Good Evening."

I thought the he would never stop talking. Every time you run into church folks, they either want you to come to something or buy a dinner. I didn't even remember him. How could he possibly remember me? Hmm. Knowing my aunt, she probably had told everyone about me before I got there.

Sunday morning, I was feeling a little churchy so I decided to check out the program at my aunt's church. The church was packed wall-to-wall. I couldn't find a place to sit. There were chairs in the aisles and they were filled up too. The choirs stand and pulpit was opened to guest choirs and their pastors. I finally spotted my aunt and took a seat by her.

I could see a look of astonishment upon her face as I made my way down the aisle. She motioned for the little boy next to her to scoot down.

"Rita? Baby what are you doing here?"

"I thought everyone was welcomed in the house of the Lord?"

She smiled and held my hand. The choirs stood in the choir stand as they awaited the director's signal. The musicians started playing and I immediately spotted Brother Jackson on the guitar. Funny how I didn't see him before. Hell, you can't miss his big butt. I must say he was sharp for a big guy. Clean cut, too.

After service, I joined my aunt in the dining area for dinner. The food was okay, but everybody at church can't cook. Brother Jackson walked up and gave my aunt a big hug and kiss.

"How ya' doing Sis. Ola Mae?"

"Fine baby. How are you?"

"Blessed and highly favored."

You ever noticed that saved folks have to get religious with every little thing? Blessed and highly favored? Why couldn't he have just said, 'I'm fine'? Boy, I tell you about church folks.

"I'm glad that you made it Sis. Rita."

"You know my niece?" my aunt asked.

"I remembered her from the last visit. We ran into each other the other day and I invited her to service. So did you enjoy yourself, Sis? Rita?"

"Service was nice, Bro. Jackson. Thanks for the invite." I answered.

When he walked away, my aunt looked over her glasses and smiled. I knew what kind of looks that was and I wasn't feeling it.

"I think somebody likes you," she said.

"Who? Bro. Jackson? Auntie he's gay."

"Gay? Girl, that boy is straight as a pole and single as a slice of cheese."

"So what does that have to do with me?"

"Look here little girl. Every single woman in this church wants a piece of Bro. Jackson."

"Why? He's fat."

"I know your momma taught you better than that. He's a good man. A man of God. See that's how you messed up the first time. You made a judgment solely on looks and how good he was in bed. It's not all about that.

"Yeah, I know. But he's still not my type."

"Huh! He may not be everything that you want. But I bet he's everything you need. Think about it."

My aunt was wise and I never took her advice for granted. She may have been right, but I didn't know anything about this man. Besides, he was just trying to be friendly. We never established that he liked me.

I passed Bro. Jackson as I exited through the sanctuary. He was in the middle of a rehearsal so I didn't bother saying bye. After putting Sarah in her seat belt, I could hear someone calling my name.

"Sis. Rita. Wait a second."

Bro. Jackson extended his hand and presented me with his business card. He then shook my hand and thanked me for coming out.

"If you ever need anything, give me a call."

"I'll do that," I responded.

"I mean anything."

"I got ya'."

I tossed the card into my purse and pulled out of the parking lot. He just stood there watching, with a dumb, confused look on his face. By the time I got home, I was exhausted. I popped in a movie and swiftly drifted off to sleep.

For some reason, I felt exuberant the next morning. I don't know if it was the makeover, Sunday's sermon, or my morning coffee, but I felt great. I hustled all day and even worked through my lunch. I was determined to get back on track by the end of the week.

By Wednesday, I was all caught up. Thanks to overtime and taking my work home, I was a free agent the remainder of the week. Around mid-afternoon, I received a call from my aunt. She informed me that Bro. Jackson was interested in my case.

"What case, auntie?"

"You know. The situation with Jeff."

"You told him about that?"

"Well, we were talking about you and…"

"When?"

"Huh?"

"When were you talking about me?"

"At Bible class Tuesday night."

My call was interrupted by a beep from another call. I had a disturbed client on the other line and had to discontinue my current call.

"I'm sorry auntie. I have to take this call. I'll call you when I get home."

"You do that, baby. As soon as you get home."

I couldn't believe that my aunt was discussing my business with a total stranger. I didn't know anything about him and now he knew all of my business. How could he be interested in my situation? What did he want to do, pray for me?

That evening, I checked my purse for his business card. "Derrick Jackson- Attorney at Law", it read. He sure didn't look like a lawyer. I called my aunt to find out what was said.

"I just told him that your husband had another wife and you wanted your marriage cancelled," she said.

"It doesn't just work like that. I'm already taking care of that situation."

"Yeah, but he's really good, Rita. He probably could work out some really good prices for you. Just call him, Rita. I already told him that you would."

"Well I guess I don't have a choice now do I?"

"Not really."

After hanging up from my aunt, I brewed me a nice, hot cup of coffee. I contemplated calling Bro. Jackson for a while. My hands were shaking as I dialed his number. Why was I so scared to call him? Maybe because I was afraid of being judged.

"Hello?" a deep voice answered.

"Hi. Brother Jackson?"

"Yes."

"This is Rita Bridges. Sister Ola Mae's niece."

"Oh yes, Rita. How are you?"

"Wonderful."

"I talking with your aunt and she informed me that you might need legal representation."

"I might. I'm not sure yet."

"Well I don't know your full case, but from the little information she gave me, you're definitely going to need representation."

"So how much is it going to cost me?" I asked in a sarcastic voice.

"Sis. Rita."

"Rita." I interrupted.

"Rita. It's not about the money. I just saw an opportunity to help a sister in need."

"A damsel in distress?"

"Whatever you want to call it. Look, if you're not interested, that's fine. I'm sorry I wasted your time. I just want you to think about one thing. You called me. You dialed my number for some reason tonight."

"I may need representation. I'm not exactly sure on what my case is, yet."

"I tell you what. Maybe we could meet for coffee, say, tomorrow? We can discuss the facts then."

"You know. You shouldn't mix business with pleasure."

"I'm not. This is business." he answered in a very serious manner.

"Okay. Tomorrow at two o'clock."

"I was also wondering if you would join me for dinner the very same evening?"

"Is that for business?"

"No pleasure."

"I like how you don't mix the two. Coffee for business and dinner for pleasure. That's real smooth."

"So what do you say?"

"I'm usually not hungry after coffee."

"Fair enough. I'll see you tomorrow, Sis. Rita."

"For coffee?"

"Coffee only."

I should have known that his slick ass was up to something. I guess he figured he'd get a little business before and a little ass afterwards. Nope. Not happening. He was barking up the wrong tree. I had a little diva attitude going for myself and there wasn't one fox that could sly me. That whole church thing he had going for himself didn't fool me. Some of the biggest dogs were in the church.

I gathered my marriage license and other important documents that Jeff and I had. I wanted to be fully prepared to discuss the legal issues of my rigged marriage. Jeff and I had investments together that was actually my money with his name on it. I was at risk of losing a lot. Not to mention that Jeff bought my house and it was in his name.

I was afraid of starting over. I wouldn't be completely broke, but I hated the thought of Jeff gaining most of my assets. I knew in the back of my mind that he was somewhere in New Orleans, figuring out a way to cash in on my hard-earned money.

Needless to say, I wasn't going down without a fight. I was going to stop Jeff or stop trying. Hopefully Bro. Jackson was the answer to my prayers. And hopefully this answer wasn't going to costume a fortune. Life's a gamble.

11
TAKING CARE OF BUSINESS

The phone nearly startled me the next morning as I prepared to go into the office. People usually don't call my house that early in the morning unless it's a bill collector looking for Jeff.

"Hello?" I answered.

"Mrs. Bridges. Hi. This is Pete, the private investigator."

"Pete, hi. I thought that you had quit on me and skipped town for a second."

"I know that I'm two weeks behind schedule, but I got some documents I need for you to look at."

"Well are you in the city?"

"Yes."

"Can you meet me at my office in an hour?"

"I'll be there."

"Thanks."

I rushed Sarah to school and flew to work, eager to see what was discovered. This was it. The truth. Pete couldn't have had better timing. He was going to provide valuable information for Bro. Jackson to determine how serious my case was.

I asked my secretary to hold my calls and inform me when Pete had arrived. I opened the blinds to let a little sunshine in my office. Just when I pulled off my blazer there was a knock at the door. It was Pete. What do I pay my secretary for?

"Come in, Pete. Did you stop at the front desk?"

"She was on a call. I slipped right past her just to see how good I was."

"So tell me. How good are you?"

"I'm worth every penny your father paid me."

He slapped a thick folder on my desk. It was packed with addresses, phone numbers, bills in Jeff's name and so on. There were even medical records and credit reports. The investigator had tracked records as far back as nineteen-eighty.

"This is incredible. How did you find all of this?"

"I'm good at what I do. It was easy actually. Business officials in the south aren't as attentive as up north. They're nicer, more laid back and gullible. Made my job easy."

"So what did you make of all this?"

"Wait there's more." He pulled a brown envelope from the inside of his jacket. It was filled with pictures.

"Who are these people?"

"Jeff's other family. He has a wife and two kids."

"I already know. He knew her in high school and…"

"She was lying, Rita. They met in their early twenties. The two boys are ten and eight. And most importantly, they were married two years after you."

"After me?"

"Yes. They were together for years before they actually got married."

"So why would she lie?"

"Money! He told her about you and all of the assets that were in his name. It was a scam from the beginning, Rita."

"So how do I get out of this?"

"Well, knowing that you're the one who's legally married to him, you have the upper hand. I suggest you contact a lawyer immediately."

"I already have. We're meeting at lunch."

"Well. It looks like fate is working in your favor."

"Maybe so. We'll see."

Two o'clock arrived and I had been waiting impatiently at the coffee shop. I didn't recognize Derrick when he walked in. He wore a jogging suit and sneakers. I had never really taken a good look at him. He was actually quite handsome.

"Good afternoon, Mrs. Bridges."

"Soon to be Ms. Bridges."

"I take it you have some new information."

"Sure do."

I told Derrick what the investigator had told me. He gave me tips on how to handle the situation for the time being. He assured me that I definitely had a case and that the divorce would be simple.

"All I want is to be free of ties to this man."

"Then maybe you'll take me up on dinner."

"Maybe."

"You don't have to be afraid of me. I don't bite."

"That's too bad. I do." I laughed. For a moment. "I'm sorry. I forgot that you were saved."

"So what does that mean?" he asked.

"I don't know actually. Do you date?"

"Just because I'm saved doesn't mean I can't date. I'm still human. I do the same things that you do."

"So do you like to dance?"

"Hey. This is business not pleasure."

"I'm sorry. So what's the next move?"

"I'm going to review these files tonight, and then I'll call you to discuss where we stand."

"Okay. I'll be waiting."

Derrick walked me to my car and bid me a good day. When I approached the stoplight, he pulled up next to me and honked his horn. I rolled down the window to see what he wanted.

"I dance pretty well actually. Tomorrow evening? Six o'clock?" he smiled as he awaited my response.

"Make it seven. I have to take my daughter to a sitter."

There was nothing about this man that enticed me. I knew nothing about him and yet I was so interested in knowing everything. He was a bit peculiar, but that was okay. He wasn't Jeff, and so far, that was good enough for me.

My mother called to check up on me. She acted as if she was interested in the case, but she was more interested in Derrick. I was certain that my aunt had told her all about him.

"So how's your new friend?"

"He's not a friend, mom. I barely know the man. He's an associate. I hired him to do some work for me. That's all."

"That doesn't mean that you're not interested. I hear he's a fine young man."

"I doubt he's anything to write home about mother."

"So what did you find out about Jeff?"

"Good things. Great things actually. It's all working in my favor."

"Well praise God."

"Praise God."

"How's Sarah?"

"She's fine mom. How are you?"

"I'm doing pretty good for an old lady."

"Well that's good to hear."

"You know I've got a birthday coming up."

"I know mom. I thought that you were supposed to wait until someone brings it up?"

"Well just in case you forgot, it's a friendly reminder."

"Thanks mom. I won't forget."

My mother was good at dropping hints before her birthday. She wanted to make sure that everyone remembered. Wouldn't be surprised if she mailed gift suggestions. I only had a week to figure out what I was going to buy her. She was just so damn hard to please. I had to really get creative on this gift. This was her first birthday without my dad and I know that she would probably be on the downside.

That night, Derrick and I had a great time dancing. We found a nice little club that had Friday night steppers sets. Derrick was a good stepper. I wasn't as skilled and kept stepping on his toes all night. I'm sure he was pissed. I would have been. He had on some nice shoes. They were all scuffed up at the end of the night.

"Maybe we should sit down. I keep stepping on your feet. I'm terribly sorry."

"It's no problem. They're just shoes."

"Yeah. Expensive shoes."

"Expensive shoes that can be cleaned. Don't be so hung up on material things, Rita. Look past the shoes. Just follow the feet inside of them."

After that, I was stepping like a pro. I guess that I was so concerned about messing up his shoes that I couldn't concentrate on dancing. It turned out to be a good evening and I really enjoyed Derrick's company. He was a very interesting man. He had an interest in perforating arts and actually danced his way through law school. I know. Sounds gay doesn't it? Actually, Derrick was in tune with himself and very secure with his manhood.

While slow dancing I could feel a little something poking between the two of us. I had had a glass of wine but I wasn't drunk. He slid his hands down my lower back in an attempt to pull me closer. Oh yeah! He was straight, alright. I don't know if he meant for me to feel that or not, but his soldier was definitely at attention.

"Having a good time?" He whispered in my ear.

"Yes. A very good time."

"So maybe we can go out again someday?"

"Maybe. If you act right."

He looked at me and lifted my face with his index finger. Our eyes locked and before I knew it, he planted one on me right there on the dance floor. It was so romantic that I thought I was starring in a movie. I could feel him grasp me as I stumbled back a little. Damn big boy! Didn't know it was like that!

I was speechless after the kiss. I didn't utter a word on the ride home. He sure as hell shut me up.

"Is everything okay, Rita?" he asked.

"Everything's fine."

"Why so solemn?"

"No reason. I'm just thinking about tonight."

"Did I do anything wrong?"

"No. Not at all."

"If I did, you would tell me, right?"

"Yes. Now nothing's wrong."

"I don't know if I told you or not but you look extremely lovely this evening."

"You told me, but it's good to hear it again."

"I bet men approach you all of the time."

"Actually, no."

"Well I can't see how anyone can surpass all of this beauty. You are genuinely gorgeous."

"Why thank you."

"And I'm not just saying that because I want a second date."

"I know."

He walked me to the door where I wished him a good night. I didn't extend an invitation into my house and he didn't ask either. He kissed the back of my hand and thanked me for such a lovely evening. After that kiss on the dance floor, I was certain that he was going to put the moves on me. That's what most guys would have done. Some would have even attempted to come in. Derrick, on the other hand, was different. He was truly one of a kind.

I had a delivery to my house the next day. It was a bouquet made of chocolates. I mentioned to Derrick at the coffee shop how much I loved chocolate. I wonder how he had it delivered so fast. It had a card attached to it that thanked me again for a nice evening. He was obviously very attentive. He was more interested in me then what I could do for him. I called him up, right then, to thank him for the candy.

"You're welcomed. You told me that you liked chocolates so I went from there."

"That was really sweet of you."

"I have some things about your case that we need to discuss. Is there somewhere we can meet?"

"If you like, we can meet here. At my house."

"I don't want to impose. We can meet at the coffee shop."

"Well, you see, my daughter has a cold and I didn't want to bring her out of the house today."

"Oh. I'm sorry."

"No. It's okay. That's why I was telling you to come here."

"I guess it'll be okay. I won't be long."

'It's alright. Just come right over. You remember the house right?"

"Obviously, if you just received the candy there."

"Oh yeah. Duh."

I straightened up around the house before Derrick arrived. I had a pot of coffee brewing while I checked on Sarah in her room. She was fast asleep. The cough syrup that I had given her must have been strong because she was knocked out.

The doorbell rang and I greeted Derrick at the door. The look on his face was a little sterner than the previous night. I guess he meant it when he said that he didn't mix business with pleasure.

"So what do you have going on?" I asked.

"It turns out that Jeff owns a house in New Orleans, two restaurants, and a nightclub."

"Wait a minute. I'm confused."

"Disregard everything that his wife, Tina, told you. She lied. He also has an apartment building here in Chicago."

"What? Where?"

"Across town, over west. The bad news is that he drew money from your assets to buy all of this."

"Which means that everything was accumulated over the course of the marriage?"

"Exactly."

"So what did he have before I met him?"

"Nothing. He was plum broke. That's why he was so quick to move to Chicago and marry you. To him, you were a walking dollar sign."

"Wait a minute. What was the address to this nightclub?"

As Derrick called out the name and address of the nightclub, my jaw fell to the floor. It was the same club that Jeff claimed to have been working at. No wonder why he was so interested in putting in extra hours at the club. Bartending my ass. I can't believe that chump.

"So where does this put me?"" I continued.

"In a win-win situation, we hope."

"We hope?"

"A case like this can take time. Anything could happen between now and then."

"Anything like what?"

"You might decide to take him back."

"Number one, he's not trying to come back. And number two, I wouldn't want him back if he was."

"I hope that's a solid statement because once he's summonsed to court, he's going to try to come back."

The thought of Jeff coming back made me want a little liquor in my coffee. I was so disgusted by the thought of him. I was more concerned about the man sitting in front of me. Even though he was plump, his sincerity and professionalism made him sexy as hell. He was so serious, but also laid back, both at the same time.

"Would you like some coffee?"

"Well I promised I wasn't going to stay long. Maybe I should go."

"No. Stay. If you're not in a hurry."

"Not entirely. I think I'd like a cup of coffee,"

We ended up talking for hours. Our conversation went deeper than Jeff and mine ever had gone. He talked with such dignity and assurance. He was such a man. Yeah. That's it. He was a man.

"I am so into you right now, Rita."

I blushed at the sound of that. I had never been so flattered in my life. He made me feel as if it was a privileged just to be in my presences.

"Really," he continued. "I'm mesmerized by your beauty."

"Okay. If you say so."

"I've over-stayed my welcome. I should go."

"No. It's been a pleasure."

"Thank you, but I must. I have to stay on your case and review the facts."

"Right."

I escorted him to the door in hopes that we could have a replay from the other night. Unfortunately, he didn't kiss me. We shook hands and he went about his way. He was a gentleman and a scholar among many. The more he turned away, the more turned on I got.

After waking up Sarah for a bathroom trip, I nestled into bed with a good book. After only reading a few pages, I was fast asleep. The phone rang loudly in my ear and startled me.

"Hello?" I answered.

There was a long silence. Then I could hear wind in the background. Whoever it was were either driving, on a pay phone or in front of a fan.

"Hello?" I insisted.

"Rita, don't hang up. It's me, Jeff."

"Well, well, well. Look who crawled from under a rock? How may I help you Jeff?"

"I know it's been a long time since we talked. I just called to say I'm sorry. I never meant to hurt you. It was an accident."

I could feel the tours pouring from my eyes. I never wanted to relive that night again. The night my husband almost killed me. Hearing his voice took me back instantly. All of the pain came rushing back at once.

"Rita. Are you still there?"

"What do you want me to say, Jeff? You tried to kill me."

"I didn't try to kill you. I was angry so I threw something."

"No. You tried to kill me. You wanted me dead."

"Rita, baby. I love you. You're my wife. I would never try to do anything like that. I just want to come home. I want to come home to my family."

"You are home, Jeff."

The next sound that he heard was the dial tone. I couldn't allow him to go on with the escapade. I was fed up. And the funny thing about it all is that he didn't have a clue as to how much of the truth I knew.

I was so shaken up after the call that I needed someone to talk to. I picked up the phone in an attempt to call my mother but somehow ended up calling Derrick. It was two o'clock in the morning and I didn't think that he might have company.

"Hello?" he answered with a yawn.

"Derrick?"

"Rita?"

"I'm sorry I called so late. I just needed someone to talk to."

"It's alright. What's wrong?"

"I just received a call from Jeff. He's trying to come back."

"Didn't I tell you? He moved faster than I expected, though. What did you say to him?"

"I basically just told him, no, and then hung up on him."

"You didn't tell him what you know, or anything about the case did you?"

"No. Nothing."

"Good. We need him to stay as content as possible. Next time you talk to him, tell him that you'll think about it."

"Hell no!"

"You don't literately have to mean it. This is just to keep him under control and off your back until he gets his summons to court."

"Oh. Okay."

"Are you going to be alright?"

"I'm just a little shaken up."

"Do you need me to come over?"

"As much as I would like that, it's late. Get some rest. I'm sorry to interrupt your sleep."

"Anytime, princess."

"You're sweet. Goodnight."

"Goodnight."

I really needed that. I needed a kind, sweet, gentleman to clean up the mess that this asshole made. Jeff didn't know what he was in for. I was going to have this jerk tied up in so much litigation that his grandchildren will still be paying for it. Now I'll admit, he might have had me going two years ago, but this was a new me. I wasn't taking his shit anymore.

The next morning, I surprised Derrick by attending morning worship. Service was pretty good but I was really going to impress him. One thing about Derrick that I liked was that it was the simple things that caught his eye. I was always so used to men expecting gifts, surprises and royal treatment.

Derrick was one of those people that were just happy to be alive. It didn't take a lot to make him happy. I admired that about him. Maybe what I've been looking for my whole life was right under my nose all along. I looked around the church and noticed all of the women giving him the goo-goo eyes.

Once service was over, the women flocked to him like seagulls to breadcrumbs. It amazed me to see women compete for the attention of one man. One plain, average everyday Joe. These women had grown up in the church with him and watched him grow from a boy to a man. They all could see his good qualities as if he wore them like a handbag.

"I see someone's grown quite fond of Bro. Jackson," a voice said from behind. My aunt was standing there smiling from ear to ear.

"Okay. Okay. You were right. Is that what you want to hear?"

"Not really. But it will do. How's the case coming along?"

"We're preparing to go to court now. It won't be long before it's all over."

"Let5's hope not," Derrick interrupted. "I can't marry a woman who's already married to someone else."

I grinned and playfully slapped his shoulder. My aunt gave me that look and walked away to leave us alone.

"Derrick, you are so crazy."

"Yes, Rita. I'm crazy over you."

"If you say so."

"If you say so," he responded mockingly.

"I'm going to get out of here. I'm taking my mom out for dinner."

"Can he go, mommy? You can go. Let's go. Everybody. He can go." Sarah volunteered.

"I'm sure Mr. Jackson has something to do today, Sarah."

"Actually, I don't. If you don't mind, I'd love to join you, Sarah and your mother for dinner. It'll be my treat."

"Who can turn down that offer? Let me call my mother and inform her that there's going to be a fourth party. She might want to put on her good wig."

Can you believe this? A man that actually wants to meet your mother? And to think, we're not even dating. Oh he got major brownie points for that one. He needed to start like a Derrick's School of Gentlemen or something. The world definitely could use more like him.

At dinner, Derrick impressed my mother with his in-depth knowledge of the Bible. It seemed as if he knew the book in and out. I drew my attention to Sarah so he wouldn't notice that I knew so little. I couldn't tell you squat about the Bible. I was without a doubt, a heathen.

"Rita, you're so quiet. Are you okay?" my mom asked.

"I'm fine mother. I'm just glad that you're having a good time."

"Oh I am. Derrick here is such a gentleman. And I just love to meet a young man of God. It truly has been a pleasure, son."

"Likewise," he replied. Then he looked across the table and winked at me.

Sarah seemed a bit interested in Derrick, too. When it was time o pat, she actually gave him a hug. The only man she had ever hugged was my father. I could see a sparkle in my mother's eye while she watched Sarah run to him.

"Bye. See you later. Bye. See you later. Bye." Sarah responded.

"Goodbye sweetie. Sweet dreams."

It's something about a man that catches your child's attention. I never wanted Sarah to have any bad experiences with men. I didn't want her to grow up and associate men with abuse. Derrick was a positive man that I didn't mind her knowing.

Normally, I wouldn't bring a guy around my child, but this was different. First of all, he wasn't my boyfriend. He was actually just a friend. Secondly, he was someone that my aunt knew and spoke highly of. Technically, he was a friend of the family. A friend who just so happened to want me divorced just as much as I did. And he was willing to wait.

I really respect the fact that Derrick hadn't attempted to get me in bed. And after meeting my mother, I had developed a whole new level of respect for him. Sad to say that I was waiting for it all to backfire. It was just too good to be true.

Why do women do that? Often times, we've been hurt so much that we don't recognize a good man when we see one. And when we get one, we don't appreciate him. Bottom line, I had recognized me a man, and I was keeping my eye on him.

12
FINAL ANSWER

I knew when Jeff had been summonsed to court because he started calling me like crazy. Everyday I had a message threatening to kill me or whip my ass. I could have sworn that he was begging to come back, just a few weeks ago. It amazes me to see how a brother can show his ass once the truth had unfolded.

Don't get me wrong; I'll be the first to admit that he had me fooled. Yeah, had my nose wide opened. But I promise you; I would be a fool for love no more. Falling for Jeff was like playing Russian roulette with my life. I was so close to losing everything. I could only hope that the judge would save my life.

I had been touching bases with Derrick on a regular to keep track of my case. Our court date was in a few weeks and I was already growing impatient.

"Hold your horses, Rita. It'll all take place in due time." he assured me.

"In due time? I'm dying here Derrick. I need to know what might happen."

"There's only one man that knows for sure and that's the Man upstairs."

"The suspense is killing me."

"No. Jeff is killing you. You still love him. You've just come to terms that he's poison to you."

"You may be right. Silly, huh?"
"No. I've been there, done that. I know how you feel."
"I thought that you were never married."
"It's true. It was an old girlfriend."
"So what happened?"

Derrick volunteered his story about an ex-girlfriend who really had him sprung. She was an older woman, who of course, taught him all of the tricks in the bedroom. After falling head-over-heels in love with her, he finds out that she was a lesbian and just trying to make her lover jealous. It was all a desperate attempt to win her back.

"You may not feel like it's the same, Rita, but it's close."
"I don't think so. Nothing can compare to the pain I've endured."
"I guess you're right. That was the worse hurt I've ever felt. I thought that it related to your pain."
"There's no hurt or pain like being cursed, raped and beaten by the one you love."
"Hopefully winning the case will take away some of the pain."
"You sound sure of yourself. Do you think that we're really going to win?"
"I don't think. I know. What I don't know, exactly, is what you'll win besides the divorce."
"What are we asking for?"
"Everything. When we're done with him, I want him to be lonely, broke, and in jail."
"As a matter of fact, put him under the jail."

We laughed and joked at the thought of Jeff being under the jail. Seemed silly, but it loosened the stiff atmosphere. Everything around me had been so serious lately; work, Sarah, the case. I was holding my breath to see what the outcome would be.

I had to stay ahead of the game at work until my court case. I wasn't exactly sure if I would have to miss days at work or not. This required me to work through my lunches and do overtime in order to keep up. According to Rick's last visit, I was one foot out of the door. He again expressed his feelings over a phone call to the office one day.

"How's things at CRI (Candy Records Inc.), Rita?"
"Everything's going well."

"Did Linda in the marketing department present her plans for the launch of the new artist?"

"She did, but there were a few discrepancies. She's tying up the loose ends now."

"Great. So how are things with you?"

"Everything's fine. I have a court case coming up. Wish me luck."

"You don't need it. It's karma, Rita. Payback was bound to come around sooner or later."

"I guess you're right. So how's New York treating you?"

"Shitty ass hell. I hate it here. The people are rude, the streets are dirty, and the smog is a mother."

"Oh, so there's no place like home, huh?"

"You got it. Chicago and New York are very similar. One just has more people."

"And far better artists, too, huh?"

"I won't say all of that. I've discovered some phenomenal talent since I opened at this location."

"I heard that new release by the young girl from Brooklyn. She's bad."

"That she is. She'll be platinum real soon. I see it already."

"Impressive. I'm glad that things are working out for you."

"I'm glad that they're working out for you, too. I haven't forgotten that you were skating on thin ice. I'll be in Chicago next month to check on things. You better be on your P's and Q's. When I made you CFO, I took a big risk. Please don't make me regret it."

"I won't, Rick."

That was a hard promise to keep. Rick had left some big shoes for me to fill. I was going through some troubling times and barely able to keep my head above water. Everything came down on me at one time.

I was at the kitchen table going over some important papers when I realized how much money Jeff had actually cashed in on. He was going to leave me plum broke. He probably had a plan to get me fired, too. I cried the whole night away. By sunrise, my eyes were swollen shut. I had to put a cold compress on them to make the swelling go down before work.

"Mrs. Rita, is everything okay?" my secretary asked."

"Yes, Lupe. Why do you ask?"

"You're all puffy. Looks like you've been crying or something."

"It's allergies. I get them every year."

"Should I run to the drugstore and grab you some medicine? You have a staff meeting in an hour."

"I do?"

"Yes. You sent the memo out two weeks ago. Remember?"

"Oh yeah. That's right. It must have slipped my mind."

I forgot. Once again I had lost track of my day-to-day business priorities. I swear. It seems like there's never enough hours in a day. I made a sad attempt to get myself together before the meeting but I failed. I could read everyone's expressions and know that they could see right pass my plastered smile.

My meeting was interrupted by an emergency phone call. I had no choice but to take the call. I returned in a rush and panic.

"I'm sorry everyone. This meeting will resume at a later date. It's a family emergency."

As much as I hated to say those words, I had no choice. My mother was in the hospital. It appears that she fell down the stairs and broke her leg. I vacated the building immediately to see her. Although it was just a broken leg, I couldn't help but think about losing her, too. And in the midst of it all, I was sure that someone was on the phone calling Rick to complain about my performance.

At that point, I really could have cared less. Everyone that wanted me out of the door were just haters. When it came to my work, I always went above and beyond excellent. Candy Records had just gotten spoiled with me going over the top. Now that I was doing just enough, there was an issue.

I rushed into the emergency room in a panic. The nurse told me to take the elevator to the fourth floor. There, I found my mom in bed with her leg all bandaged up. She was watching television and eating applesauce. She was just as happy as could be.

"Mom. What in the hell were you doing?"

"Cleaning the ceiling.

"Cleaning the ceiling?"

"Yeah. I was trying to knock the cobwebs down and I fell. I'm alright, though."

"How bad does it hurt?"

"Well they've got me all drug up so I really don't know."

"How long do you have to stay?"

"They're getting ready to put my cast on now. I have to stay here tonight. Hopefully I'll be able to go home tomorrow."

"That's when you're coming home with me."

"Why? I'd be fine at my own house, thank you."

"I need to keep my eye on you for a while."

"You have work, Sarah, and the case. You already have enough to worry about."

"Yeah, and now you. Just can't stay out of trouble can you?" I laughed.

"You know me. I'm always into something."

I spent the rest of the day with my mom. I called Sarah's school to inform them that Shawntee would be picking her up. Her name was already on the emergency list. All she had to do was show some identification. I knew that Shawntee would feed her dinner and let her play with the other kids, so Sarah was in good hands.

Now my mother? She was lying. Her house stays spotless, so I know damn well it wasn't any cobwebs on the ceiling. She obviously was doing something else. I waited until she drifted off to sleep before I attempted to ask her the truth.

"Mom. Are you awake?"

"Huh?"

"Mom. How did you break your leg?"

"That darn pigeon."

"What pigeon?"

"The pigeon in the attic."

"In the attic? What were you doing in the attic?"

She was silent. She was too into her sleep for me to ask her now. I knew that shaking her would partially wake her up from the nap.

"Stop shaking me, girl." she mumbled.

"Mom, what was in the attic?"

"Those damn pigeon. He was trying to tear my papers to shreds."

I knew that getting the whole story out of her was going to be a challenge. I decided to let her get some sleep while I headed to her house. Once again, I was on a snooping rampage. Why must my mother always send me through this? Why must she be so stubborn?

At my mother's house I retrieved the ladder from the basement and climbed into the attic. She was right, there were pigeons everywhere. They probably had scared the shit out of her and she fell. There was stuff everywhere, but I don't know how it got up there. There's no way my parents could have put it there when they moved in.

I opened a dusty trunk where there were old pictures of a bunch of white people. They were all dressed up in ball gowns and suits. It was a black and white photo from the eighteen hundreds. The house must have been gutted out before remodeling and no one removed anything from the attic.

I guess my mother was just curious of what was up there. But why would she lie about it? This was no big deal. Then, at the bottom of the trunk, I saw a familiar face. It was an old picture of my mother. There I found a lot of pictures in a pile. They were pictures of my mother with different men. Some were even naked pictures. They were pictures from back in the sixties.

Surprisingly, none of these men were my father. My mother was dressed like a prostitute in most of the pictures. I couldn't believe my eyes. I was certainly hoping that they were all Halloween pictures and she was just in costume. I knew better. It was true. My mom was a hooker.

This secret never came out and I wondered how many people in the family knew. I even wondered if my dad ever knew. How could this me? She was a married woman. Why would she do such a thing? As much as I didn't want to, I had to ask.

The next day I when I picked my mom up from the hospital, I presented her with the pictures. I waited until we got in the car and slapped them right in her lap.

"Explain this to me please."

"What were you doing in my house? And snooping at that?"

"I knew that you were lying about your leg. Now explain, please."

"I don't have to explain anything to you."

"You need to tell me something. Were you prostituting?"

"No. Yes."

"Oh my God! Why?"

"Your father was in the service and had been stationed in Pakistan. I hadn't seen him in months. That's when I got word that he was sleeping with the women over there and spending his money on them. We were broke and the holidays were coming up. Your father didn't send the money for food or toys for you and your sister. I had to make due."

"There were other ways. You could have worked a second job."

"I could have, but I enjoyed it. Your father wasn't home and I was young, sexy and horny. I wanted to live that lifestyle for a while."

"Are you listening to yourself? You're saying that you enjoyed it."

"Well, all of my clients were friends of your father before I started whoring. I already knew them and felt more comfortable being with them. They bought us groceries, paid the mortgage, and one man gave you guys a Christmas."

"So you're sitting here trying to tell me that you did it for us?"

"I did."

"The sound of that sickens me."

"I'm sorry that you had to find out this way, Rita. I never meant for you to know."

"Does anyone else know?"

"No. Your father never even knew. I think Ola Mae figured it out, but she never said anything about it."

I drove the rest of the way in complete silence. If it isn't one thing it's another. She really expected me to just accept that bullshit? I guess I had no choice. I was grown and my mother was not taking care of me anymore. My father was dead so I guess it didn't matter to him either way. I was tempted to take my mother home, but I had already announced that she was going home with me. She was feeling bad enough and I had made the situation worse.

I fixed her and Sarah a light dinner and afterwards had to get her ready for bed. If she were home alone, she would have had a hard time bathing herself. That was a job and a half. My mom was pretty heavy and because of her leg, it was all dead weight. She struggled into the guest bed and with the click of the remote control, she was out cold.

I could hear the phone ringing in the other room and immediately ran to answer it. After such a long day, I didn't want to run the risk of waking Sarah or my mother.

"Hello?" I answered.

"Hi, Rita?" a voice asked on the other end.

"Yes. This is Rita."

"Hi. This is Derrick. Remember me?"

"Very funny. What's up?"

"Nothing. Just hadn't heard from you in a while. Is everything okay?"

"Sort of. My mom fell and broke her leg today. She's going to be staying with me for a while."

"Is there anything I can do to help?"

"No. Thanks anyway, though."

"No problem. Look, I was wondering if you've got word from Jeff, lately?"

"He's been calling and making threats. He blocks his calls. That's how I know it's him."

"He should be in Chicago in a few days. We go to court next Thursday."

"We do? It simply slipped my mind."

"How could something this big slip your mind?"

"Just the date. Of course I remember what could possibly be the biggest day of my life."

"Well I just wanted to forewarn you of what could happen. Jeff may appear at your doorstep. You be careful."

"I'm a big girl. I can handle myself."

"Just be careful, Rita. If you need anything, call me."

"Will do. Thanks Derrick."

It was good to know that Derrick was more concerned about my well being, rather than getting in my drawls. He was one of the few, honest, Christian brothers that I knew. I truly admired that about him. He was indeed one-of-a-kind.

My mom was a hassle over the next few days. She called my job all day long, requesting that I make frequent stops to the house on my breaks. Unfortunately, I was unable to follow through with all of her requests. I worked downtown, and it was impossible to run home during my breaks. I didn't understand what the problem was. I fixed her breakfast before I left for work everyday. Her lunch was prepared and in the refrigerator. All she had to do was microwave it. What's so hard about that?

"On your way home dear, could you grab a pint of banana ice cream?" she would ask.

"Mom, you have a broken leg, not a baby. Where do you get such bizarre tastes from?"

"It's the television. Every time a commercial comes on advertising food, I get hungry."

"Well read a book."

You would not believe how hard it is to find banana ice cream in Chicago. Not banana fudge or chocolate chunky banana; just plain ol' banana. My mom was wearing down the last nerve that I had left. And poor Sarah. She had become my mother's personal butler. "Sarah get grandma a glass of water. Sarah get grandma some tissue. Sarah scratch my back." I was sick of it.

It was almost at an end when the doctor announced that her leg was healing. He didn't take the cast off, but he did give her some tips on how to take care of herself when she's home alone. As independent as my mother was, I thought she'd be ecstatic about going home. Instead, she hung her head and sobbed.

"What's wrong mom?"

"Nothing."

"Something's wrong because you're too quiet."

There was no response. My mom never grieved in front of me, but I knew that she missed the company of my father. She didn't have many friends and her daily activities were limited. I was at a dead end with her. Hell, I couldn't read her mind. She was going to have to tell me what she wanted.

"Look, mom. I know that you don't want to go back to your house and stay by yourself. What is it that you want to do?"

"Just take me home. I'll be fine," she said with a hint of sarcasm."

"No you won't. Would you like to come live with me and Sarah?"

"No, honey. You have your own life."

"You're part of it. What is it that you want mother?"

"I want to sell the house."

"I just bought you that house."

"I know, Rita, but it's just too much house for one person."

"And where do you plan to live, mother?"

"In an apartment."

"You want to sell your house to live in an apartment? What sense does that make?"

"Makes a lot of sense. There are more people around that I can get to know."

"How about getting to know your neighbors that you have now?"

"I don't like them. Too many white folks for me."

There it was. I almost forgot whom I was talking to. My mother always was prejudice. Let her tell it she wasn't though. Whites didn't intimidate her she just didn't like them. Why? Who knows? She probably didn't have a legitimate excuse, herself. I always tried to tell my mother that Blacks weren't the only people on the face of the Earth, and she couldn't isolate herself into one little, Black community forever. But believe me, she tried.

"How about we buy you a condo instead?"

"Ain't that what you used to live in?"

"Yeah."

"Child, please. A condo ain't nothing but a big ass apartment with a mortgage. Doesn't make sense to me."

"What if we sold the house and bought a two-flat on the southside? You could stay on the first floor and we'll rent the second floor to another widow your age."

"Now that sounds like a plan."

Finally, something that satisfied my mother's wants and needs. I explained to her that she would have to wait until after the court case was settled. I already had enough on my plate. Needless to say, I was pleased with the final decision. I certainly did not want my mother moving in with me. I was still young, and I did not need my mother all up in my business. She was already in it enough.

I finally had time to sneak away and see Derrick before court the next day. He invited me over for dinner. Sarah stayed with my mother so that she would have some company over the weekend. It was my first time seeing Derrick's place, and I must admit, I was impressed. He had a pretty cool pad for a bachelor. If I didn't know any better, I would have assumed he had a woman living with him. His house was spotless.

He had prepared a candlelit dinner for two in his elaborate kitchen. There was soft music playing in the background, and he had a unique electronic mural that covered an entire wall. It was a picture of a sunset on the beach. It was like actually being on the beach. I could feel the wind blowing across my face and the warm from the sun resting on my cheek.

"Where did you get this mural?"

"Neat isn't it? I ordered it online."

"How does it look so real?"

"That's actually a screen that's covering the wall. Look up at the ceiling. There's a projector in that box that shines the picture onto the ceiling. There's also a fan, that makes the breeze, a light that generates the warmth of the sun, and a recording that makes the crashing sound of the ocean waves."

"Excuse my French, Derrick, but get the fuck out of here."

I know that I probably sounded like an ass, but I was amazed by such a creation. I was sure that it cost him tons, but I wouldn't dare ask. Believe it or not, I did have some class about myself.

After dinner, Derrick escorted me to his basement where there was an actual dance floor. We danced for hours under the disco lights. He was pulling out all of the tricks for this date. I had never had a man go to such an extent to please me. I felt like a true queen. He was my king, Sarah was my princess, and Jeff was my royal pain in the ass.

"So are you nervous about tomorrow?" he asked.

"Of course I am. Jeff was what I thought would be my one and only true love. He did everything that was unthinkable to me. And now, I finally have to face it all. I haven't seen this man since he put me in a coma. I don't know how I'm going to feel when I look into his eyes."

"Just remember one thing, Rita. God is on your side. He'll carry you all of the way."

"Will he catch me if I pass out?"

"No. I think that's my job," he laughed.

"Derrick, you're so nice to me. Why?"

"Stop asking why, and start asking why not. Don't you feel that you deserve all of these things?"

"I do, but..."

"Shh...."

He picked me up and carried me to a nearby sofa. I melted like putty in his arms as we engaged in a romantic kiss. Somehow the music had changed with the mood. All of a sudden there was no disco. The c.d. had switched to soft jazz again. I hated to break up a good moment but I just had to ask.

"Did you set your c.d. like this, intentionally?"

"Of course I did. And everything was timed perfectly. Now be quiet and make love to me."

Now that's what I'm talking about. I thought he'd never ask. For a minute there, I was starting to worry. A brother wasn't putting the sex moves on me and most men don't pass this up. I don't care how saved he was, even preachers didn't pass this up.

We worked our way down to our underwear and then he slowed down. Apparently, I was in a rush, so I slowed down, too. By the time I starting working down his boxers, we completely stopped.

"What's wrong?" I asked.

"I said make love to me, Rita. We can make love without being sexually intimate."

"So you don't want to have sex?"

"Rita, what I feel for you are far beyond sex. I don't care how short of time it's been I love you. I want to spend the rest of my life with you. But until tomorrow, you're still a married woman."

"How do you know that you love me, Derrick?"

"You've everything that I've ever prayed for. If perfect was a human, you would be it."

I don't know about you guys, but that was good enough for me. He said and did everything that was right. But did I love this man back?

"I don't know if I know love anymore, Derrick."

"You don't have to. It'll find it's way back to you sooner or later. I just want to be the one to show it the way."

"You know. Just when I think that you can't amaze me anymore; you do."

"That's what I'm here for; to amaze. Hopefully I'll do the same thing again in that courtroom tomorrow."

I rested easy in Derrick's arms that night. I didn't have a care in the world. He was everything that I wanted and needed in a man. I just didn't want to introduce any of my drama into Derrick's life. I had to break free of my past before I entered into the future.

The next morning I had the jitters. Derrick was more bold and confident than I was. He straddled into the courtroom with a bold look of unconcern. I sat there nervously biting my nails until it happened. The doors flung open and Jeff came stepping into the courtroom. Sweat beaded up on my forehead as I heard his footsteps approaching me from behind.

"Don't turn around," Derrick ordered.

He could tell by the sweat that I was going to have a breakdown in a few seconds. I closed my eyes and attempted to keep it together. Not once did I look into Jeff's face. I couldn't even tell you what color suit he had on. I just kept my eyes closed and my mouth shut. I could hear the judge ask Derrick if I was okay.

"You honor, my client has to live through this for the rest of her life. It's a big step for her to be here today. A step towards starting a new life."

Those words were more so for me than the judge. I could feel Derrick's eyes locked on me he said it. I knew that I had to build up enough courage to testify against Jeff. When I was called to the stand, I opened my eyes, took a deep breath, stood up, turned and stared directly into Jeff's eyes. He grinned in a daring attempt to scare me.

"God is with you," Derrick whispered in my ear.

I closed my eyes and prayed that God would carry me to the stand. He did. When I got up there, I took another look at Jeff and that stupid grin on his face. My mind flashed back to the day I met him and then fast-forwarded to the day he put me in the hospital. I opened my mouth and sang like a mocking bird. Everything that I could remember about our relationship, I told; the good, the bad and the deceit.

At the end of my testimony, court was in recess. I joined Derrick at a nearby coffee shop for some tea. I was so shaken up that I burst into tears.

"Rita, stop crying. It's all over now. You've gotten past the tough part."

"I know. It's just…"

"What, Rita?"

"I don't know what came over me. When I looked into Jeff's face, I felt nothing but rage. I wanted to kill him."

"We must not think that way, Rita. Just pray and ask the Lord to renew your strength. It's almost over."

We finished out tea and walked around downtown to enjoy the cool, crisp air. I called to check on my mother and Sarah before going back into the courtroom. I walked in and noticed Jeff talking to a woman and two teenage boys. It was her. Tina. I couldn't believe that he would bring her to court with him. How stupid could he be?

"Derrick, it's her."

"Who?"

"Tina. The other woman he's married too."

I took a good look at her and was in total disbelief. She looked nothing like I'd imagined. She was short and fat. She had long hair but it was extremely raggedy and wild. If it weren't for her weight, I would have thought she was a crack head. I mean she did look a little strung out. Good for him. I hoped that they would grow old together. They were perfect for each other; two fools.

We all rose as the judge read the verdict. I closed my eyes, bowed my head, and prayed. For that moment, I heard nothing but my prayer. I prayed to God for true happiness and peace. I prayed for someone that would be a good husband to me and a father to Sarah. I prayed that my past would be erased and that all would be forgiven. I didn't want to hold a grudge over anyone, especially Jeff. Life was certainly too short or grudges. As I said "Amen", I could hear the courtroom applaud.

"What? What does this mean Derrick?"

"It means we won. You're a free woman."

And there it was. I was free as a bird, and apparently well off. I was able to regain control of all of my assets and write Jeff off in my book forever. Since the nightclub and two-flat building was purchased with my hard earned money, the judge granted me full ownership.

I reached over and gave Derrick the tightest hug ever. I wanted to do more, but we were in court and that would have definitely been inappropriate. On the way out, I picked up my pride and put it on my shoulders as I reached out my arm and shook Jeff's hand.

"Until we meet again, Jeff." I was wearing the grin now.

I called my mom immediately from the car to tell her the good news. She said that she already new that it would be a good outcome because she had prayed on it. She was already in the process of baking me a victory cake.

"What kind is it, mom?"

"German chocolate. Your favorite."

"I'll bring the ice cream."

I asked Derrick to join me in my celebration at my mom's house. He agreed to come under one condition.

"What's that?" I asked.

"Marry me." He reached in my jacket pocket and retrieved a little blue, velvet box. Inside, was a two- carat diamond ring. My jaw dropped.

"That was in my pocket the entire time?"

"I slipped it into your pocket when we returned after recess. I was hoping that you didn't find it before the verdict. So what do you say?"

"Yes." It was a no-brainer. This time, I was marrying for love, not lust.

We arrived at my mom's an hour later and walked into a big "Surprise." All of my family and friends were there and a couple of unfamiliar faces, too.

"Rita, I'd like for you to meet my mother and father."

"Nice to meet you, Rita. We've heard a lot abut you. Congratulations on your engagement," his mom said.

"You all knew?" I asked.

"Everybody knew, dear," my mother started. "He asked me for your hand in marriage last week."

"You mean to tell me that you were actually able to keep a secret, mother?"

"This was too juicy to tell."

"And you, Shawntee. My best friend?"

"He swore me too secrecy," she responded.

I couldn't believe that Derrick was able to pull this off. I was swarmed with a host uncles, aunts, nieces and nephews, all from his side of the family. It was definitely a new beginning and I was off to a good start. A man who could pull this many tricks out of his hat was a keeper.

That evening, I received a call from Rick. He wanted to congratulate me on my success. I was glad to hear that I was officially off of his shit list. He had gained a new level of respect for me.

"I tell you, Rita. You're tough for a young woman. There should be more out there like you," he said.

"There are. Some just don't know it yet."

"You may be right. Take care of yourself, Rita, and congratulations on your engagement. I'll be in touch."

"Talk with you later, Rick."

At the end of the party, my mother announced that she had a special gift for me. She directed everyone's attention to the outside patio where she had a pit fire burning.

"What's she gonna burn, her marriage license?" my aunt laughed.

My mother presented me with a big, white box with a bow on it. I opened the box and inside I found the pink dress that my father had bought me when I was a little girl. As much as I loved that dress, I knew what I had to do. I walked over to the pit and tossed the dress right into the open flame. Everyone was silent for a moment. No one quite knew what was going on.

"What in the heck did you do that for?" my aunt Ola Mae interrupted again.

"Because, auntie. I'm a real woman, and real women don't wear pink."

I grabbed my purse, my daughter, and my man, and waved to the crowd as we rode off in the moonlight. It was done. I had become a real woman, and there was no turning back!

ABOUT THE AUTHOR

P.D. Carter is founder and CEO of True Potential Inc., a non-profit that provides career assessment for minority women. Aside from writing, she is also a lecturer and public motivational speaker. She is a world-renowned philanthropist who supports aspiring writers, speakers, and entrepreneurs. P.D. Carter studied Architecture at Florida A&M University & continued her education at Chicago State University where she received her Bachelor of Science in Business and Administration with a concentration on Marketing. She resides in Chicago with her family, where she continues to inspire for generations to come.

Printed in the United States
54985LVS00003B